ID667819

Micki felt as if she was being sung to by a siren, and she stepped back a bit.

"Why move away?" Angela asked directly. "Don't you like this?" she whispered, blowing swift wisps of air through Micki's hair, pressing her breasts against Micki's body, slipping her hand up under her shirt, fingertips playfully teasing.

In reply, Micki's hands began to slide down Angela's back and she caressed her. She buried her face in Angela's hair, their bodies swaying to a rhythm all their own. Micki had forgotten where she was, so gripped was she by the sudden waves of pleasure that swept her body. If we weren't on a dance floor, she told herself, we'd be making love right now.

Other books by Shelley Smith

The Pearls

Horizon of the Heart

EDGE
OF
PASSION

Edge of Passion

Shelley Smith

RISING TIDE PRESS

Rising Tide Press
5 Kivy Street
Huntington Station, NY 11746

Copyright © 1991 by Shelley Smith
All rights reserved.

Without limiting the rights under copyright reserved above, no part of this publication may be reproduced, or transmitted in any form or by any means (electronic, mechanical, photocopying, recording, or otherwise), without prior written permission of the publisher.

Printed in the United States

All characters, places and situations in this book are fictitious and any resemblance to persons (living or dead) is purely coincidental.

First printing April, 1991
10 9 8 7 6 5 4 3 2 1

Edited by Lee Boojamra and Alice Frier
Book cover design and illustration by J KOLSTAD & CO

Library of Congress Cataloging-in-Publication Data

Smith, Shelley
        Edge of Passion / by Shelley Smith
                p. cm

ISBN 0-9628938-1-1

                        91-60161
                         CIP

For Elisabeth

CHAPTER 1

Worn windshield wipers skidded across the glass, smearing the fine mist which was falling. Micki looked toward scrub pines bending in the raw east wind and promised herself she'd have the wipers replaced tomorrow. She was relieved as she saw the Orleans rotary just ahead. The long drive from Boston to Provincetown was nearly over.

Soon Micki cruised past Eastham and Wellfleet, traffic surprisingly light for Friday, and began the last stretch of the trip between Truro and Provincetown where the curved arm of Cape Cod seemed to provide safe harbor, even on as bleak an evening as this.

In Truro, she turned off the highway onto Route 6A, driving past the long rows of tiny wooden cottages that lined both sides of the narrow road. They looked like bleached match boxes sitting on the sand. Soon windows would be thrown open to fresh sea air. Canvas lawn chairs in bold stripes and bright colors would be set up on scrub grass lawns and sandy beaches. In the shallow waters off shore, day sailers and motor boats would be moored as the Cape moved into yet another summer.

This early weekend in June, though, the season hadn't quite begun. It was a good time to visit P-town, Micki reflected, no matter what the weather. She'd been putting in too many hours at Hewitt's, the department store where she worked, and a weekend out of the city, away from her job, was just what she needed.

On impulse, she'd left her assistant in charge that afternoon. Business had been slow all week, and though Micki might have used the day to catch up on paper work, none of it was urgent. After leaving work, she stopped off at her apartment for the overnight bag which was always packed, a habit acquired from her many buying trips to New York. She put on a pair of Levis, a comfortable sweater, quickly chose slacks, a jacket, other clothes, and was soon on her way.

Now she was almost there. Approaching Commercial Street, catching sight of the Provincetown Monument, she realized that the rain had stopped. Twilight was fading into dark, but she smiled at the sight of a wide band of crimson stretching out across the horizon, surely a promise of clear weather for tomorrow.

Driving to Ariel's Guest House in the West End, she noticed new shops and restaurants, sightseers meandering up and down the narrow street, townies and tourists alike passing time on newly painted benches in front of the Town Hall. No doubt about it, Micki thought, after a frigid winter and the prolonged coldness of a New England spring, P-town was coming back to life.

The second floor waterfront room she'd rented was spacious and pleasantly furnished. Micki opened a glass slider leading to the deck, listened to the incoming tide, followed the running lights from a shore bound vessel, and made her plans for the evening. She'd shower, change clothes, have dinner. Nothing fancy, she decided. Then she'd make her way down to the Blue Moon Cafe.

Any woman who was thirsty or wanted company knew the Blue Moon, the oldest women's bar in Provincetown. The blue neon crescent that hung from the wrap-around porch of the weathered Victorian structure was vintage art deco. It outlined the silhouette of a long-haired woman leaning back against the gently curving line of a quarter moon. She seemed to welcome all.

When Micki opened the wooden screen door and stepped inside that night, she began to search for familiar faces--one in particular, her friend Noelle Daniels. She felt sure that Noelle would be working the weekend, and she was disappointed that she wasn't there.

Good friends now, once they had been lovers, Micki's first, she recalled. They'd met through a mutual friend when Micki and her husband Guy had first separated. The attraction between Micki and Noelle was mutual, sudden, and joyous, and it wasn't long after their meeting that they became lovers. Now, some twelve years later, Micki still savored memories of the months they were together.

Unfortunately, angry memories of the divorce hadn't faded either, she reflected, especially where her son Mark was concerned. She'd anticipated that child custody would be the most difficult aspect of the divorce, but what she hadn't been prepared for was the swiftly damning evidence her husband's lawyer had amassed on what he called the "lesbian issue."

Since she hadn't accepted or acted on her feelings for women until after she'd left Guy, she knew it hadn't been an issue in their marriage. But Guy had used it. His lawyer had produced photographs, had called witnesses Micki was sure had been paid to follow her and Noelle into the women's bars they visited, and the judge had awarded Guy full custody of the boy.

Bitterness and grief over the loss of her young son, then just ten years old, evolved into a long period of depression for Micki. The guilt Noelle felt for having been a factor in the court's decision didn't help either. Soon Micki was encouraging her to accept out-of-town engagements, to pick up her own life, to move in a new direction. Micki felt too fragmented to offer Noelle what she deserved.

But now, Micki usually made a point of touching base with Noelle by stopping in wherever she was singing. She knew the clubs Noelle played in New York and on the Cape, and naturally, she knew where to find her in P-town.

At the sound of a familiar voice, Micki turned and saw Noelle standing beside her. She returned the affectionate hug and kiss Noelle offered.

"I'm so glad to see you," Micki exclaimed. "I was beginning to think this was your night off."

"Friday?" Noelle asked. "Never!"

They walked toward the long bar that ran the length of the room. The polished mahogany took a graceful turn in front of glass sliders that opened to a deck where women gathered for conversation or a dance.

"Summer madness," Micki observed, smiling at the women dancing on the hardwood floor a few feet away. "A bit early in the season, isn't it?"

"Not for business," Noelle replied.

"Of course, that's still the name of the game," Micki said cheerfully.

She draped her arm comfortably around Noelle's shoulder. "P-town agrees with you, you're looking wonderful."

Noelle turned to the mirror behind the bar and took in the image which reflected the two of them.

"We had good weather most of the week, so I've just managed to get an early start on my tan," she replied lightly.

"No," Micki persisted, "it's more than that. You've done something with your hair, haven't you?"

Noelle laughed. "I had it *cut* yesterday. Same style you've seen for years, though maybe a bit more extreme than usual, that's all." She brushed a few stray strands of black hair back from her forehead. The short haircut accented her high cheekbones and dark eyes.

"We've got to expect changes now that we're on the far side of forty," Micki began.

"*Stop* it," Noelle protested, "I'm not writing myself off as ancient history, why should you? It's all in the genes anyway. My grandmother looked and *felt* great into her eighties. She's *my* model for the next three or four decades! Besides, I wouldn't say you have anything to worry about," Noelle said admiringly as she looked at Micki.

In contrast to the lavender shirt and black slacks which Noelle wore, Micki had changed from her jeans and sweater to a shimmering turquoise blouse, oyster white slacks, a dove grey jacket. Her clothes clung to her body like a seductive caress. To Noelle, in spite of the cool weather, she seemed hot that night, restless. The only thing that wasn't steamy about her was the expression in the cool grey pools of her eyes.

Her full lips had been glossed a deep plum and a touch of rouge softened broad cheekbones. Her hair, as usual, was simply styled, a long, straight blonde fall, cutting a sharp, even line at her shoulders.

4

"We're weathering the journey rather well," Micki concluded cheerfully.

"I'd say so," Noelle replied. "Now what else is happening with you? Anything interesting?"

Micki knew the intent of Noelle's question, and though she had several romances in the years they'd known each other, she was still unattached. But as Micki appraised the crowd at the Blue Moon that night, Noelle thought that it was only a matter of time before that would end. Micki was one of those women who had always struck Noelle as a natural for love, even though she hadn't found what she was looking for yet.

"Not much," Micki responded, a trace of a smile crossing her lips. "And you and Jessie, I take it, are just fine."

"Oh, yes," Noelle said, contentment reflected in her brown eyes. "We've got a great apartment, top floor, sky lights, sun deck, water view, quite nice! Jessie runs the food concession here. Since they stop serving at eight, she still has plenty of time for her writing."

"And when do I get a copy of that album of yours?" Micki inquired. "I've been looking for it everywhere."

Noelle sighed. "We thought it would be released by now, but with a firm as small as Kore Music, distribution can be a problem. From what we've been told, my guess is early fall."

"That's all right," Micki assured her. "No business runs like clock work. The important thing is that you and Jessie have gotten this far."

The album was a collection of songs composed and sung by Noelle to Jessie's lyrics.

"Of course," Noelle agreed, "but naturally we're excited to see it."

When Noelle and Jessie began working together two years ago, they were pleased to discover how a single line from a lyric could inspire melody and, likewise, how a phrase of music could influence the creation of poetry. They relished the satisfaction they'd experienced in their collaboration and felt fortunate in realizing the completion of their first project. They saw it as the beginning of something very special which they hoped to continue.

Over the blare of the music, midway down the bar, a loud voice called out. "Hey, pretty lady, what's *your* heart's desire? Me or a drink?"

Micki smiled at the woman walking their way. "Why don't I start with a tall gin and tonic? We'll work up from there. What'll it be for you, Noelle?"

"Just coffee," she answered, "I go on in a few minutes."

"Now that's a lot of woman," Micki said emphatically, as the bartender walked away to fill the order. "True love and happiness...for someone."

"You'll *like* Lana," Noelle said cheerfully, "everyone does."

When she returned with the beverages, Lana folded her arms on the bar and leaned toward Micki.

"I didn't mean to come on that strong, I just get carried away when I see a good looking woman. I'm not the promiscuous type," she said with conviction. "Name's Lana, by the way."

"I'm Micki, Lana, and thanks for the compliment."

Lana stood up to her full six feet, smiled broadly and put her hands in the pockets of her chinos.

"My pleasure," she said in a friendly voice. "Making women feel comfortable and relaxed is an important part of my job. I don't just mix drinks at the Blue Moon, Micki, Noelle can tell you that. I've got more responsibilities here than most people would want to handle. I like to think of myself as sort of a combined goodwill ambassador, earth mother, therapist, and all-around friend." Her expression became thoughtful as she continued. "These big shoulders have had a lot of gals crying on them, but I guess I can take it."

Micki smiled and nodded in acknowledgement of Lana's revelations.

"My only request is a small one, Lana," she said agreeably. "Any chance of turning down the sound system?"

"That's one thing I *can't* do; it's against company rules." Lana shrugged her shoulders and wiped her hands on a bar towel. "Besides," she said, raising her eyebrows, "ships at sea might get lonely."

"Not if they hear *that*," Micki replied quickly.

"Lisa Stansfield's "This Is the Right Time?" Hey, I *like* that song," Lana said, doing a two step behind the bar.

"I'll have to get used to it then," Micki responded.

Lana's face broke into a smile that was dazzling. She propped her chin on a large open palm, leaned across the bar and said, "You're all right, pretty lady." Then she turned and walked down to the far end of the bar.

Micki and Noelle watched Lana entertain a group of women who had clustered around her as they patiently waited for the bottles of chilled beer she served them. She reared her head back and laughed loudly, then clapped her hands as if to send them off to school.

"The stories I could tell you," she said, returning to Micki and Noelle. She chuckled, ran her hand across her forehead, brushed wisps of short, curly hair back from her eyes.

"One of those kids claims we've got a celebrity in the house tonight. Out on the deck. Angela Hall, the TV reporter. What do you think she's doing at the Blue Moon? Research for one of her specials?" She gestured to the large TV bolted to the shelf behind the bar.

Just then the slider from the deck opened and all three women watched as the young reporter who was familiar to anyone who tuned in to Channel 8's Evening News suddenly became the center of an admiring circle of fans. Her smile was ingratiating, and its effect achieved what she wanted. Several women stepped back, allowed her to pass, and she walked slowly to the bar.

"Now's my chance to meet her," Lana said excitedly. She glanced in the bar mirror and with a quick gesture turned up the collar of her kelly green T-shirt. "See you later, ladies."

"TV cameras don't do her justice, do they?" Noelle asked as she glanced at Micki.

Micki smiled and shook her head. "How often do media celebrities like Angela Hall visit the Blue Moon?"

"Not often," Noelle replied.

"Then I wonder what it's all about," Micki mused, her gaze drawn to the woman now standing at the bar.

7

She was dressed simply in a white linen shirt and white slacks. Thin gold chains circled her neck. Her dark almond skin and thick black hair seemed to glow in an aura set off by the whiteness of her clothes.

Obviously enjoying the attention she was receiving, she ran her tongue over her lips and raised thinly arched black brows at a comment someone near her had made. She lowered thick lashes over deep brown eyes and shook her head no.

Micki imagined that she did that often, said no to some invitation or other.

Angela smiled at Lana, who rocked back and forth on her heels, obviously spellbound, and accepted the glass of wine which had been poured for her. Then she gazed in the direction of Micki and Noelle. The expression on Micki's face revealed that she was intrigued by the young woman. For a brief second, it seemed that their eyes met and held, but someone had stepped in front of Angela, blocking Micki's view of her, so who could say if they had noticed each other?

"It's hard *not* to look at her, isn't it?" Noelle asked, aware of Micki's fascination.

Suddenly Lana stood in front of them, her expression grim.

"I've seen her type before, appears so in control, but underneath that pretty smile, she's bad news, ladies. I can feel the vibrations all the way down here."

"Like I can feel the pull of the tides from the full moon?" Micki asked skeptically.

"You can, you know," Lana answered. "We're moon children, all of us. Daughters of the moon we are."

"What else is new?" Micki asked.

"Lunar rhythms are there for us to recognize," Lana said intensely.

"For lunatics," Micki said softly to herself.

"Don't mock the power of the moon," Lana insisted. "Especially not with her in the room."

"What *are* you talking about?" Micki asked impatiently. "She's young, talented, full of life, that's all."

Micki glanced her way, noticing that now Angela was involved in an animated conversation with two women who stood close to her. Long, slender hands that seemed to have a life of their own gestured in the hazy air. Angela brushed her dark hair back from a high forehead and smiled at the women. She appraised the crowd objectively, but time and again, her eyes turned toward Noelle and Micki. Someone spoke to her and she laughed, her warm throaty tones carrying all the way down to where they were sitting.

A few minutes later, when Angela walked back out to the deck, Noelle and Micki tried to pick up where their conversation had left off.

After a while, just as Noelle was about to go backstage, she caught a glimpse of white out of the corner of her eye and realized that someone was standing next to Micki.

"Do you want to dance?"

Micki quickly glanced at Noelle, then swiveled her bar stool around so she was facing Angela Hall.

"Would you like to dance?" Angela asked again.

"You're kidding," Micki responded in surprise.

"Why?" Angela smiled as she waited for an answer.

"Dance to that?"

"Why not? Everyone else does."

Micki shook her head no. "If I even tried, I'd end up spending a week in traction."

Angela stepped closer to Micki. She touched her on the arm, gently. "How about a slow dance?"

Micki was intrigued by the invitation, flattered. She studied Angela, then spoke.

"You'll never hear one in this place," she said with conviction.

Angela smiled. "I'll be back," she said.

"I'll be here," Micki answered, "but don't count on the music."

"We'll see," Angela answered as she walked away.

Micki turned back to Noelle and Lana. Noelle couldn't repress her smile, but Lana looked solemn.

"Trust my feelings. Stay clear of that one," Lana said earnestly.

"She probably asked me to dance on a dare. Tease the geriatric crowd." Micki's mocking tone was a defense.

Lana shook her head. "She's had her eyes on you. I've been watching her. And don't kid yourself, pretty lady, you know what she wants, don't you?"

Lana waited for Micki's reply, but then customers called out to her and she suddenly left.

"It's a moot point, isn't it, Noelle?" she asked. She shrugged and laughed, "They never change the music here, do they? Besides, aren't you due on stage soon?"

"Yes, as a matter of fact in about five minutes. Can you take care of yourself?" she asked teasingly.

"Haven't I always?" Micki replied.

For Micki, the sudden, subtle change in the music didn't register with her until she saw Angela walking her way.

"Ready for our dance?" Angela asked.

"How'd you manage that?" Micki replied.

"I just can't take no for an answer."

Micki laughed. "Okay," she said, "we're on our way."

When they stepped onto the dance floor, Angela said, "Know who I am?"

"How could I not?"

"And who are you?"

"My name's Micki."

Angela put her arms around Micki's shoulders as Micki lightly touched her waist.

"Micki who?"

"Questions already? D'Allessandro."

"Thanks, I like to know who I'm dancing with. Hold me," Angela implored, stepping closer. "Is Sarah Vaughan's 'Misty,' slow enough for you?" she asked. She began to hum the melody, singing phrases from familiar lyrics.

Micki felt as if she was being sung to by a siren, and she stepped back a bit.

"Why move away?" Angela asked directly. "Don't you like this?" Angela whispered, blowing swift wisps of air through Micki's hair, pressing her breasts against Micki's body, slipping her hand up under her shirt, fingertips playfully teasing.

In reply, Micki's hands began to slide down Angela's back and she caressed her. She buried her face in Angela's hair, their bodies swaying to a rhythm all their own. Micki had forgotten where she was, so gripped was she by the sudden waves of pleasure that swept her body. If we weren't on a dance floor, she told herself, we'd be making love right now.

Who am I kidding, we *are* making love, Micki admitted to herself. And then suddenly, in the gentlest of touches, Micki felt herself enveloped in a second skin. When she looked at Angela, she was surprised to see that her eyes were glistening, with joyful emotion or tears, Micki wasn't sure.

"So sudden," Angela said, drawing Micki even closer.

Micki had to try to break the mood; it was much too intense for her.

"Like the song, do you?" Micki asked, quickly running the tip of her tongue across her glossy lips. She laughed helplessly at her own inane question.

Angela told her later that with that question, that ripple of laughter, she felt herself falling, falling into the laugh, the sound of her voice, the warmth of her touch.

"Yes," Angela murmured, "don't you?"

Micki answered Angela's question with her eyes, then her fingers lightly stroked Angela's body and they moved more to the rhythm of each other than the music.

Angela's lips left kisses, wet, quick, on Micki's neck. Micki buried her face once more in a tangle of thick black curls, breathed in a tantalizing essence of exotic perfumes.

"How are you doing?" Angela whispered in her ear.

"I don't believe this," Micki answered breathlessly.

Angela smiled and took Micki's hands in her own, bringing them to her lips where she kissed her fingertips.

"Let's be by ourselves," Angela urged.

"Here?" Micki asked. "With all these people?"

"You want that, don't you?"

They were only a few feet away from the back alcove of the room, a dark, quiet corner.

"Over there," Angela urged, "we'll be alone, just for a few minutes..."

Micki wanted to pull back. It was all happening too fast, but she knew they were already over the line. When Angela stepped back into the darkness, Micki followed. As they kissed, Angela grasped Micki's hands and guided them over her body.

For Micki, time seemed to stop as Angela's pleading, moaning sighs, the sounds of her pleasure, beginning softly, seeming to soar, then finally obliterating the music that played on, held her captive in a passionate spell. Then their bodies rested quietly, one against the other. Micki watched Angela carefully. She looked as if she was awakening from a dream. She pulled Micki close.

"Did you know it would be like this for us?" Angela asked, her voice thick, as if heavy with sleep.

"No, of course not," Micki said softly, incredulously.

"I did, I felt it from the first moment I saw you. Leave with me now, come back to my room."

Micki shook her head back and forth as she brushed Angela's hair back from her eyes.

"No." Micki's breath was hot as she spoke the word.

"You don't mean that," Angela insisted.

"Yes, I do," Micki answered with conviction.

Micki wasn't sure of exactly why she didn't leave the bar with Angela that night, but just then she felt overwhelmed by Angela's intensity.

Angela leaned back against the wall holding Micki's hands, stroking her palms with her fingertips. "You don't want to leave things like this, do you? How can you?" she asked plaintively.

Then Micki had a glimmer of what was behind her own resistance. It wasn't that she hadn't had sudden encounters before, though, in truth, they were few and very far between. And it wasn't the difference in their ages, though Micki wasn't ignoring the factor of Angela's youth. It was a mixture of feelings that emerged primarily from her own cautious nature. She questioned Angela's neediness, her motives, and wondered about the need for power she sensed in her.

Micki wasn't willing to risk a further encounter with this just yet, even for a night of love such as she knew they would have. She was determined to turn the situation around, to break the mood Angela was intent on maintaining.

"Angela, slow down," she implored. "What just happened with us here and on the dance floor isn't *connected* to anything else--"

She insisted, "Yes it is, it's our beginning--"

Micki's voice was firm as she spoke. "I don't know about that, Angela, but I'll tell you this much, it was one hell of a dance, one that *I'll* never forget."

Wanting to end the conversation, she led Angela back across the dance floor. As she looked at her, she saw her expression quickly change. A few minutes before, she was vulnerable in her passion, needy. Now her lips wore that on camera smile as her eyes gazed coolly at the crowd. She was in complete control of herself, and her demeanor toward Micki was haughty, impersonal, almost arrogant.

"Order me a Perrier," Angela said sharply, as they approached the bar.

Angela continued to cast her eyes about the crowded room. When it seemed that no one was watching her, she turned to Micki and said tersely, "You're not leaving me."

Micki was shaken by Angela's words, as Angela's expression conveyed the intensity of her command. Micki had already decided not to comply, but rather than respond, she ignored the comment and ordered drinks from Lana, who let Micki know by the expression in her eyes that she was aware of all that had transpired.

"Here you go, quench your thirsts on these," Lana said.

A group of women standing nearby recognized Angela and so she raised her glass and smiled at them.

"Always on in your business, right?" Micki asked, wanting to change the mood.

"It depends," Angela said, shrugging impatiently. She stepped back from Micki, conceding an unexpected defeat in what she had presumed would be an easy conquest.

"*The* Angela Hall," Micki continued. "Quite a success, aren't you? Imagine, when you were born, I was probably already out of college and working to put my husband through law school."

"You're married," Angela said flatly. "It's a little past your curfew time, isn't it?"

"I'm divorced," Micki replied.

"Then why bring it up?"

"It's a handy reference point for me. Reminds me to make sure I'm doing as much as I can with my own life," she said emphatically.

"Are you?" Angela asked.

"I try," Micki replied. "How old are you, Angela?"

"I'll be twenty-eight in August. Can you use that as a reference point?"

Micki thought for a moment before she spoke. "Sure," she said. "I completed the retail training program at Hewitt's the summer of '63, was hired as an assistant lingerie buyer and found it, aside from making it possible to pay the bills, totally irrelevant. I was more interested in what was going on down in Jackson, Mississippi than I was in acquiring managerial skills, especially when they were limited to nothing much more than how to display the latest style in bras."

Angela laughed and Micki began to feel more comfortable now that the conversation was less threatening.

"Civil rights, yes?" Angela asked.

"That's right. I helped with voter registration one August and in '67, we went to Washington for the March on the Pentagon." Micki laughed self-consciously. "It must sound like a cliché out of ancient history now, but we thought we were going to help change the world."

"Why did you stay in retailing?"

"Someone had to pay the rent. Then, most women didn't question working while their husbands finished school. It seemed more important that Guy get his law degree, especially after I became pregnant."

Presenting Angela with family history was a distancing tactic which almost worked, but at the mention of her son, Micki felt uncomfortable and regretful, remembering the pain of the divorce, the loss of Mark.

"You have children?" Angela asked.

"A son. He lives in L.A.," Micki answered softly.

"Tell me something about *yourself*," Angela prodded, sensing Micki's discomfort. "About now...not *then*."

"I don't know what you mean," she said defensively.

"Yes, you do. Don't put me off, Micki, you'll never meet anyone like me again." There was a bit of self-mockery to her tone, but only a bit.

Her voice urged Micki to comply, but just then, behind them, stage lights lit up and Noelle's accompanist stepped out from behind the velvet curtain to a ripple of polite applause. His medley of show tunes led into Noelle's introduction.

"It's time I moved on," Angela said, "unless you've changed your mind about coming back with me."

Micki's answer was a slight shake of the head. Then with a light kiss on the lips, Angela said goodbye, turned and merged with the crowd.

Micki looked up to see Lana standing in front of her. "A lot of different stories start in places like this," Lana began.

"Stop, I'm too old for sermons," Micki interrupted.

"Stories begin," she continued, "and stories end. Once in a while, I know the ending before the story really gets started."

Micki felt apprehensive hearing Lana's words. She wanted to defend herself.

"*Nothing* is going to happen, Lana. No story's going to begin, so there's no need to worry about the ending. She's a kid, Lana, a gutsy, ambitious kid. There wouldn't even be half a chapter between me and Angela Hall."

The house lights dimmed and Micki turned to see Noelle walk briskly out on stage and acknowledge the enthusiastic applause.

Though Micki seemed to be directing her attention to Noelle's smooth renditions of current show tunes and old standards, her mind was on Angela.

Later, Angela told Micki that she'd sat alone that evening, at the far end of the bar, catching glimpses of Micki through the crowd, disappointed that Micki didn't look in her direction. She couldn't get the feel of Micki's touch out of her system, the connection she felt between the two of them. There was a moment when Angela had felt Micki's flesh reach out to her, when she'd felt the lines between the two of them dissolve so that there was only one being, one beat, one pulse. Now, Micki seemed so very far away.

*****

Jessie often stopped in at the Blue Moon when Noelle was performing, but that evening she arrived later than usual. She walked down the length of the bar looking for a seat that was free, disappointed that Noelle had already begun her set. The conversation Angela Hall began with her was one of the first things she told Noelle about when they both got home that night.

Jessie Holbrook would be the first to admit that by nature, she's a shy woman, not the type to initiate conversations with strangers or go out of her way to meet people. But when Angela Hall walked over and sat down beside her, she *was* curious. Channel 8's coverage of the news was Jessie's favorite, and though she wanted to tell Angela that she admired her work, she was hesitant about speaking to her.

She was surprised, then, when Angela began talking to her. It was a casual enough conversation, but the purpose of it was perplexing to Jessie. Why was Angela Hall asking her questions?

"A friend of mine, she's standing over there," Angela said lightly as she gestured to a cluster of women standing at the edge of the dance floor, "said you knew a lot of the women who are regulars here."

Jessie wasn't sure of how to respond, but Angela got right to the point.

"What do you know about that good looking blonde at the end of the bar?"

There were a couple of tow-headed softball players sitting up that way, so innocently enough, Jessie asked, "Which one?"

Angela gave her a saucy look and said playfully, "She's sitting by herself, the older woman, the one watching the singer so intently."

The damp weather that day had frizzled Jessie's hair. Fine, tight red curls fell about her shoulders over the navy wool sweater she wore. Her hazel eyes questioned Angela, but her response was a noncommittal shrug.

"What do you think she and the song-bird have going for them?" Angela inquired.

Suddenly, Jessie found it all amusing. She'd already decided that she wasn't about to reveal anyone's past *or* present history to a stranger, even if Angela was a celebrity. The last thing Jessie was about to announce was that she and Noelle had been lovers now for six years. And that Micki was just a friend, though true, a very special friend.

"I wonder *who* her lover is," Angela implored, glancing in Micki's direction.

"I'm afraid I can't help you," Jessie responded firmly, "I don't know much about her at all."

Angela persisted. "I've got a seventh sense about these things and I don't believe you, my friend. I'm curious about Micki, that's all. We met a while ago and I can't imagine a woman like that without some strings attached somewhere."

"Then why don't you ask her?" Jessie asked.

"Subtle inquiry's very big in my business. There's a value to discretion, know what I mean?"

Angela quickly changed the subject and within minutes she had Jessie talking about herself and her work. When Angela found out Jessie was a writer, a poet, she had her hook. She wasn't about to give up on what she felt was a connection between this woman and Micki and the singer who had just left the stage. She told Jessie she was coming back to P-town next weekend. She suggested that the two of them have lunch, and perhaps then she could read some of Jessie's poems.

"Who knows?" she asked. "I might be able to work you into a series of spots I'm planning to do later this summer on Cape Cod's artists and writers."

Jessie admitted to herself that while she was flattered by Angela's interest, she was equally curious about her fascination with Micki.

"That would be wonderful," Jessie replied, thinking that some advance publicity for the album she and Noelle had cut certainly couldn't hurt. "Angela...angel...your name suits you well."

Angela laughed. "Angels don't make news by discovering bright, upcoming, new lyricists. Reporters do. But thanks for the thought. And see you next week."

As Angela walked away, Jessie doubted that she would ever see her in person again.

CHAPTER 2

The elements that drew Angela to Micki had taken hold immediately. In the days following their first meeting, no matter where she was, no matter what she was doing, the feelings that had been aroused as they'd danced that night at the Blue Moon were uppermost in her mind. Micki's laugh, the softly assuring sound of her voice, her touch, her caress, Angela could not forget.

Later, in describing the headiness of her euphoria to Micki, Angela said she had no choice but to find a way to see her again, to assure that once more they would be together. When she talked of the days that followed their first meeting, she concealed nothing, as if in describing the details of the pursuit, she was elevating the value of the prize. Not that it took her very long to get what she wanted. Angela told Micki that she must have been ready for her, waiting for her. Perhaps. It happens that way sometimes. Passion springs up from the moment so suddenly that the only word which seems adequate to explain it is Fate.

As a reporter, it was part of Angela's job to gather routine information from various sources. After calling information, she found that Micki's telephone number was unlisted. She contacted a friend who worked in the personnel department of Hewitt's who gave her Micki's address and home telephone number. A contact at the Registry of Motor Vehicles supplied her with a description of her car and the license plate number. That was enough to go on. For now that was all she needed to know.

The following evening, wanting to see where Micki lived, she drove her sleek, silver Alfa Spider over to the Back Bay. Usually, spring takes hold quite gently in Boston, but by early June, the pale, lovely blossoms from magnolia and dogwood trees growing along the streets and avenues had faded and fallen. Now hearty, red begonias and tall flags of scarlet salvia brightened floral gardens fronting stately buildings. Beyond, city sailors cruised the Charles River, tacking east to the mouth of the Atlantic or west to Cambridge.

Angela drove down Back Street, the narrow avenue providing access to various parking spots behind the blocks of Beacon Street condominiums and apartment buildings. She spotted a burgundy Mercedes sedan, checked the license plate to see if the car was Micki's, and then proceeded to Newbury Street, where she parked, walked to a nearby bar, ordered Perrier and made her first phone call.

Angela didn't intend to speak to Micki, but to continue the quest, she needed the reassurance that she felt would be there even by hearing her voice. The phone rang several times and just as Angela was about to hang up, disappointed that Micki wasn't home, she heard a breathless, "Hello."

Angela listened.

"Hello? Hello? Anyone there?" There was a pause while the line hummed loudly.   "Hello?" she asked once more, her voice separating the word into syllables, as if that might prompt a response from the caller. Still not hearing the sound of a voice, Micki hung up.

Angela replaced the receiver, returned to the bar to pay for her drink, and soon went home.

The next evening, she decided that the direct approach would be best. Perhaps with others Angela had the patience for cat and mouse games, but before, she had only toyed with women for the pleasure of the hunt. With Micki, she wanted much more. She parked, reached for a bouquet of flowers she'd bought from a local florist, and as she was about to leave her car and cross the street to Micki's building, she spotted her. Angela watched as Micki gazed down Beacon toward the Public Garden. It was obvious that she was expecting someone to pick her up.

A few minutes later, a cruising metallic blue Toyota Celica slowed down and Micki walked quickly to the car. Angela couldn't see if the driver was a man or a woman, but she turned on her ignition, pulled out of her parking place and decided to follow them wherever they were going.

The coupe turned left, headed for the South End. Angela felt excitement rise in her as she followed them to her own neighborhood. When the car turned from Clarendon onto Tremont Street, she decided they were on their way to dinner.

As she watched the driver ease the car into an available parking place, Angela felt apprehensive. Would Micki's companion be a friend, a lover, a business associate?

Angela couldn't be sure as she watched the tall woman step out and wait for Micki to emerge from her car. They walked quickly toward a row of renovated brick buildings, and entered a basement level Italian restaurant. It happened to be one of Angela's favorites.

I wonder who she is, she asked herself. If my old friend Gary's at home, I'll be stepping in there with a date myself. And if he happens to be out for the evening, won't Ms. Micki D'Allessandro be surprised when she sees me request a quiet table for one so that I can go over the script for tomorrow's shooting. She drove the short distance to her apartment on West Newton Street delighted, by what she saw as a stroke of luck and good fortune.

Once inside, she dialed Gary's number. "How wonderful, you're home," she exclaimed. "Any plans for tonight? Want to come and have a bit of supper at the Capriccio with me? My treat, it's an expense account meal. I'm in a rush. Can you be ready in ten minutes? Great, great, *great!* Meet you downstairs in a flash. Love you forever," she said, hanging up and running to her closet, grabbing a red silk blouse, black slacks, heeled sandals.

Gary Kaufmann had been her friend long before she had moved into the apartment. In fact, he'd told her about the vacancy when one of his first long-time lovers had decided to leave Boston and accept a job in San Francisco. She'd returned the favor by alerting him to the production job he now held at Channel 8.

Angela laughed at his surprised expression when she walked toward him. She was hardly ever on time.

"Something going on that I don't know about?" he asked, crossing his arms, raising his eyebrows. "What's the hurry?"

"We don't have reservations, darling, and you know how crowded the Capriccio's been lately. Besides, I'm starved tonight. Aren't you hungry?"

She reached for his hand. They walked to Tremont Street, and a few minutes later they entered the restaurant. Louis assured them that it wouldn't be long before they'd be seated. While they were waiting, Angela searched the room for Micki and her companion. She spotted them at the back of the restaurant; they were so intent on their conversation that Micki wasn't aware that Angela had come in. Other people had noticed, Angela mused as she realized she was attracting a bit more notice than she wanted.

When they were escorted to their table, Angela chose the seat facing Micki. In the small restaurant, there'd be no way that Micki wouldn't be aware of Angela's being there.

Angela timed it then, all so carefully. She sat down, unfolded her napkin, picked up the menu, leisurely considered the choices, then turned in the direction of the rear of the restaurant, and raised her eyes to meet Micki's.

The expression Angela saw on her face was reward enough for moonlight sleuthing. Later, Micki told her how astounded she was to see Angela in the restaurant. She'd watched her on TV twice that week, found her image on the screen a mesmerizing one, and now that she was here, only a few feet away, Micki admitted that she couldn't take her eyes off her.

Micki's dinner companion, Beverly Keating, a friend of many years and assistant advertising director at Hewitt's, noticed that she seemed distracted and asked Micki if anything was wrong.

"That's Angela Hall sitting over there," Micki replied in as noncommittal a voice as she could manage.

"Yes, I saw her when she came in. What's your interest in her?" As she waited for Micki's response, the expression in her blue eyes reflected curiosity.

"I'm not sure," she said, speaking thoughtfully. "I met her in P-town last weekend...we got to talking." Micki shook her head, not wanting to reveal anything else. "She's lovely, though, isn't she?" Micki continued. "Know what I'd like to do? Send a bottle of wine over to their table. They haven't ordered anything yet, have they?"

"I don't think so," Beverly replied, chuckling. She nonchalantly ran her hand through thick auburn hair. "I'd like to hear some of the details of the conversation you two had."

Micki laughed. "I'm just in a good mood tonight. What's wrong with toasting new friends?"

"Not a thing, Micki," Beverly assured her. "Why don't you order a dry white?"

"How about the Pinot Grigio we're drinking?" Micki asked.

"It *is* good isn't it?" Bev asked, raising her glass to her lips. She smiled. "Micki, your generosity never fails to amaze me...or is it your method?"

"Don't read too much into this, Bev. After all, what's a bottle of wine? Would you help me signal the waiter? I'd like to send the wine over to Angela's table before her friend orders a bottle."

As the waiter presented the wine to Angela and Gary, Angela smiled, raised her hand to her lips and blew Micki a kiss. Micki blew a quick kiss back and raised her wine glass in a silent toast.

The meal passed pleasantly for Micki, though it was difficult to turn her attention away from Angela's table to focus on dinner conversation with her companion.

Micki and Beverly often met for dinner, which, since they both lived alone, gave them a chance to unwind after a hectic day. That evening, Beverly spoke of upcoming changes in the department. She was curious as to whether or not Micki had heard any gossip about forced retirements.

"Of course," Micki responded, "but they're not going to be restricted to advertising. Golden parachutes they're called, aren't they?"

"Gold-*foil*, you mean," Beverly exclaimed. "Sam Kramer's leaving this month. He's being given nothing beyond what's in his pension plan! The word is that management wants a new, young team...throughout the store."

Micki reached out, took Bev's hand, gave a comforting squeeze. "We don't have to worry about that yet," Micki said reassuringly. "Sam's over sixty, isn't he?"

"I'll be fifty-two next week," Beverly replied quietly. "The years pass so quickly now."

Micki spoke encouragingly. "You've always wanted your own business, Bev. Why don't you start out with a few free lance accounts? See how you like working on your own."

Conversation began to move in a more positive direction, and a short while later, as they finished their coffee, Micki wasn't surprised to see Angela heading their way.

"That was so *nice* of you to send the wine over," she said, smiling at Micki.

"I hope you both enjoyed it," Micki answered. "Let me introduce you to a good friend, Beverly Keating."

Beverly extended her hand, said hello.

"Hi," Angela responded, her on-camera smile on her lips. "It's really nice to meet you. Micki, my friend Gary and I were just talking about going out to do a little partying. You and Beverly like to join us?"

"We'll pass this evening," Micki said. "And who's covering the city while you dance the night away?"

Angela laughed. "Even hard working reporters get a night off now and then. Actually, I had a spot on the six o'clock news. Did you happen to catch it?"

"No," Micki replied, "I got home later than usual. Will the piece run again?"

"It's scheduled for eleven...unless something of importance has happened since we've been here enjoying ourselves.

"Got to get back to Gary," she said in a rapid-fire delivery. "We've just ordered dessert and if I give him the chance, he'll polish off both of them."

"Happy to have met you," Beverly said pleasantly.

24

"Same here." Then she turned to look at Micki. "It was fun last weekend, wasn't it?"

"Yes," Micki replied.

"I just can't forget about it," Angela said lightly. "Keeps popping up in my mind at the *strangest* times. Who would have thought I'd end up just loving slow dancing?" she asked dreamily, her tone changing, her voice now soft and husky.

There was nothing Micki could say, but Angela saw the acknowledgment of her words in Micki's eyes.

"You're not heading down the Cape again this weekend, are you?"

"Friday," Micki answered, deciding on the spot that she intended to make the trip two weeks in a row.

"Terrific. My car's going in for a tune-up. Any chance of Gary and me catching a lift?"

"Don't see why not," Micki responded lightly. With Angela's sidekick along, it would all be harmless enough.

"Any special place we should meet?" Angela asked.

"This neighborhood convenient?"

"Couldn't be better. I live only a few blocks away."

"Clarendon and Tremont," Micki said. "About six."

"Six sharp, it's a date. Now enjoy the rest of the evening, you two."

As Angela returned to her table, Beverly leaned across the table and purred, "I can see why you're impressed by the girl."

"Woman," Micki answered, the expression in her eyes an adequate response to Beverly's inquisitive gaze. Though in truth, in ways, Angela seemed little more than a child to Micki.

Back at home, Micki turned on the news. Angela's spot wasn't shown. She was disappointed, turned off the light and TV, tossed restlessly till sleep came.

CHAPTER 3

For the rest of the week, Angela went back to business as usual. There was no need for phone calls or ruses now. She congratulated herself on how easy it had been to make plans for the coming weekend and vowed she wouldn't give Micki the chance to reject her again.

She played with memories from their first meeting, as if they were beads on a silken cord-- the warmth of Micki's touch, the heady aroma of her perfume, the expression in her grey eyes...

Where had she seen such eyes before, Angela asked herself. Whose gaze had held the promise of so much love? She wanted Micki the first night she'd met her, she recollected, almost from the first time she saw her. She willingly succumbed to her fantasies...not of a dark corner at the Blue Moon, but of Micki in her room, in her bed...

*****

It was easy for Angela to convince Gary that a P-town weekend was what he needed to get his mind off a romance that had recently ended, especially when the ride was being provided and the company was bound to be good.

Angela was packed and ready to go when he arrived at her apartment, but before she picked up her luggage, she invited him to share the four short, grainy lines of cocaine she'd laid out on the surface of her compact mirror.

Gary joined her willingly enough, but he was surprised at the offer of the coke. Though there were rumors enough at the TV station about who did and didn't indulge, she hadn't acknowledged her own interest in drugs before this occasion. She had learned to play it safe, to distance herself from anything that was questionable concerning her professional or her private life.

"What a nice surprise," Gary said after she'd carefully cleaned the mirror and closed the compact.

"Wasn't it?" she asked brightly. "Just a little extra someone left after a party. I'm not into it, you know that, don't you? I'd heard you were so I thought I'd give it a try."

His expression was cynical. "Is that so?" he asked. "Aren't you a sweet kid? How do you like it?"

She smiled. "I'm a fast learner, Gary, remember? It's *real* nice. Just what I needed to get the weekend off to a good start. Let's get going. I don't want to be late."

She locked the door behind her, threw her keys into her bag and linked her arm through his.

They walked quickly, laughing at old jokes, tuning into each other, enjoying the brief headiness of the high they were sharing. As they approached the corner of Clarendon and Tremont, Micki was waiting for them.

"It's not six yet, is it?" Angela asked with some concern, as she slipped into the front seat of the vintage Mercedes. "My watch must be running slow. It usually keeps perfect time."

"Traffic was light," Micki said casually, "I'm a few minutes early."

"Okay!" Angela responded with enthusiasm. "You two weren't introduced the other evening, so let me do the honors now. Gary Kaufmann, meet Micki D'Allessandro. And vice versa."

"Hi," Gary said, as he climbed in back. "Real leather, what a turn-on."

Angela and Micki laughed as Gary caressed the seat. "It's so roomy! Do I have to be back here all by my lonesome? If I spot a friend, can I invite him to join us?"

"You be a good boy back there," Angela answered, "and have naughty daydreams. No stops for anyone, right Micki?"

"Absolutely," she said, making her way up Mass. Ave. to the expressway ramp. It was an easy drive out of the city. With a repertoire of jokes and stories, Gary kept them laughing all the way down Route 3. After they circled the rotary at Plymouth and crossed the Sagamore Bridge, he said, "Well, gals, it's time for a treat. And don't think I'm talking about ice cream."

Before Angela had a chance to stop him, he pulled a small pill box and mirror out of his duffel bag.

"Gary? What are you doing?" Angela asked, her voice rising with surprise. She turned quickly toward Micki to gauge her reaction.

In the rear view mirror, Micki watched Gary lift a small amount of white powder from the box and place it carefully on the small hand mirror. In his right hand, he held a thin metal tube, but it wasn't until he bent his head down over the mirror that Micki realized what was going on.

"Is this the way you always travel?" she asked.

"If I'm able to," he said, leaning his head back against the soft leather of the seat.

"How about it? Shall I pass this up your way?"

"No, Gary, put it away," Angela said sharply, turning to face him. "The least you could have done was to let Micki know what *you* were going to do."

"Sorry, I thought we'd all be fellow travelers," he said as he closed his eyes and dug his hands deep into the pockets of his jacket. "But whatever pleases the driver pleases me."

"I say we stop at the Inn in Orleans for coffee and a club sandwich. Just a quick break, all right?" Micki asked, preferring to change the subject and ignore what had just occurred, rather than let Gary know that she was shocked by what he had done.

At the Inn, they were shown to a corner window table where they viewed a fine mist moving in over the water. She could sense that

Angela was agitated, probably, she thought, by Gary's behavior. For the moment, he seemed to be in his own happy little world, and not wanting to put a complete damper on the party for Angela's sake, Micki suggested they order a bottle of wine. While they sipped on the wine and waited for their sandwiches, Micki felt herself unwinding from the tired feeling that often came at the end of the day. She looked at Angela, who was caught up in conversation with her friend.

Aside from easy affection, Angela didn't seem to be pushing anything. She and Gary probably had plans for some late partying once they got to town. Then she remembered last week's dance and she wondered what Angela *was* doing with her time this weekend.

In P-town, they inched their way down Commercial Street, the crowd of pedestrians seemingly oblivious to the cars which followed them. Micki dropped them off at their guest house, and apart from a reminder that she'd meet them at the same spot Sunday evening at seven, no plans were made.

With Angela gone, Micki felt quite suddenly alone. Rather than checking in at her room, she decided to stop off at the Blue Moon.

She kept thinking about Angela, wondering who she might be meeting, telling herself it was none of her business, trying to convince herself that there were too many reasons that it wouldn't work between them, that what happened last week was very nice, indeed, but that it wouldn't...it shouldn't happen again.

She told herself that the difference in their ages was reason enough not to pursue a relationship, but, she reflected, she'd been alone for so long...

After Noelle, there had been other lovers, but for some reason, whether it was out of concern over Mark's visitation rights, or the demands of her job, or a general distrust of relationships, she hadn't committed herself to anyone.

She'd grown used to living alone and in many ways, she liked it.

Besides, Micki felt that Angela was beginning a career that would eventually take her far beyond the local TV station where she was now doing human interest stories. She'd watched her spots carefully that week and admired the confidence she projected. She was still finding her way, that was clear, but Micki recalled several reporters who had moved on to network positions in New York after they'd achieved success in Boston. With Angela, she didn't think it would be very long before this occurred.

As she walked toward the Blue Moon that night, she repeated all of these reasons to herself once more.

The club was packed when she arrived and Micki winced at the sudden assault from the sound system which blared a hot beat.

She looked about the crowded room for Noelle, and when she didn't see her, she eased herself onto an unexpectedly vacant bar stool and waited for Lana to make her way down to her end of the bar.

"Lana," she called over the throbbing noise that seemed to shake the very walls of the building. "Any chance of getting a cup of hot coffee?"

"Coming right up, pretty lady," Lana said as she winked and gave Micki a friendly wave.

"Noelle about?" she asked, as Lana placed the mug in front of her.

"She sure is. She's taken my gal Ruth backstage to let her see the underside of show biz. When Ruthie sees that cubbyhole of a dressing room, she'll know that it's not all glamour and tinsel. I want Ruth to see things as they *are*, Micki. Think there's anything wrong with that?"

"Not at all." Micki sipped on her coffee, as amused by Lana as she had been last week when they first met. "I didn't realize you weren't a free agent, Lana."

Lana looked across the bar to Micki and laughed. "Ruth and I have what you might call an on-again-off-again relationship. She showed up last week and this time we've finally come to our senses. We're going to tie the knot, white tux, wedding cake and all. It won't be till August when Ruthie gets her two-week vacation, but you'll be getting an invitation. Just be sure you leave your address with me so we can add you to the official guest list."

"Wonderful! Congratulations," Micki said raising her mug in a toast.

"When you're in love, Micki, you wish the same for everyone you know and you see nothing but love all around you. Jessie and Noelle have never seemed happier. Even the old war horse we work for, Rose Cabral, seems content with her gal Toni. Just look around-- *everyone's* in love--or should be!

"Now how about you, Micki?" she said in a serious, confidential tone. "You're too nice a lady to be here all by your lonesome. What are *you* all about, love?"

"Me? I'm a realist, Lana, that's all. I guess you might say I missed my chances at love."

"Why? What gives you that idea?"

"Wrong time, wrong place," Micki said somberly. "Isn't that what we're talking about?"

"Maybe, but take my word, Micki. We're all realists...till we *fall* in love."

Lana waited for Micki's answer, but she offered none. Then Lana looked beyond Micki and smiled. "My sweetheart's back. Let me introduce you."

Micki turned to see Noelle standing beside a small, thin woman. Her serious expression was focused on the scene around her. As she was introduced to Micki, she looked shyly away, as if she found social situations awkward and not to her liking. Then her gaze fell on Lana, her eyes widened with affection and she smiled. She reached across the bar and picked a few pieces of lint from Lana's navy T-shirt. Lana enjoyed the attention she was being paid. She reached across the bar to draw Ruth closer, to take her hand.

As Lana and Ruth began their own conversation, Micki and Noelle were left alone to discuss how the past week had gone for each of them. It was small talk, the easy, shorthand communication of long-time friends.

Micki mentioned that she hadn't made the trip alone, but because she didn't tell Noelle who her passengers had been, Noelle was taken aback by the young, beautiful woman who stepped up behind them and wrapped her arms around Micki as if they'd known each other for years...or as if they were in the midst of a blossoming love affair.

At first, Noelle didn't recognize her, but then she recalled the sensation Angela Hall had caused at the Blue Moon the previous week.

"Micki, you're *here*," Angela cried out in a shrill, excited tone. "Gary and I had so much *fun* riding down with you."

Then she turned and noticed Noelle.

"Oh, hi," she said innocently. "Didn't mean to intrude on a private conversation. I'm sorry, really I am. I'm Angela Hall...and you're Noelle Daniels. You're the best, Noelle, right up there at the top."

Noelle's expression revealed that she was flattered by Angela's compliment, but at the same time she thought about how easy it would be to be taken in by someone like Angela. She was a pro...in all ways.

Noelle listened as Angela chattered on. "It was just so *nice* of you to bring us down. I'll have to think of something special to do in return. Maybe I'll pack a picnic lunch for the trip back. Would you like that, Micki?"

"As long as the refreshments aren't the kind your friend serves up," Micki replied seriously.

"Aye, aye, captain," Angela responded, raising her right hand to her forehead in a mock salute.

"No big date tonight, Angela?" Micki asked.

"No way. I am meeting an old friend who's up from New York for the weekend. Anyway, I've been working so hard lately, I wouldn't know what a big date was. In fact, that's why I'm here right now. My friend should be coming along any minute, if she isn't here already. In this crowd, it's pretty hard to see beyond the general crush. My, my, let us feast on all this flesh."

As Angela glanced about the room, Micki didn't take her eyes off her.

"You sure *look* as if you've got a date, Angela," Micki prodded lightly.

"You mean this shirt? You think gold's my color?"

"Any color's *your* color," Micki said with a tired, happy expansiveness.

Angela laughed. "You're sweet," she said. "Isn't she?" she asked as she turned to Noelle.

"Very," Noelle replied.

Then Angela, her eyes expressing concern, looked down at her wrist and lightly ran her finger across the face of an antique gold wrist watch.

"I meant to leave this back in my room. I just noticed that the safety clasp's broken. It was my mother's, about the only thing I have of hers. Would you mind holding onto it for me till Sunday? If I had pockets in this shirt, I'd tuck it away myself...I'd just hate to lose it."

"I'll take care of it for you," she replied holding out her hand.

"You will?"

Angela reached out, unbuttoned the breast pocket of Micki's shirt and placed the watch inside.

"Here's a safe spot," she said. "Now you won't forget it's here, will you?" she asked, taking her time at buttoning the pocket.

"I'll put it away as soon as I get to my room...which is going to be very, very soon."

"Then I'll just give you a good night kiss and be on my way," Angela said, leaning against Micki and kissing her lightly on the lips.

"Noelle," she said in parting, "You take care of my big sister here, and maybe I'll see you both some time over the weekend. Bye, you two."

Angela moved off into the crowd and was gone.

It didn't take long for Noelle to get to the point. It was only because Micki and Noelle had been friends for so long that she pursued the questions she asked. It was clear to Noelle that someone as young and beautiful and wily as Angela appeared to be, would get whatever she wanted. And if she wanted Micki, as it seemed from the beginning that she did, Noelle just wanted to be sure that her friend knew what she was letting herself in for.

"Who is this Angela Hall to you?" Noelle asked pointedly.

"Why nobody...but a lovely young woman I just happened to meet last weekend. Why? She's still a kid, isn't she? Either one of us could have a daughter her age."

"I wouldn't describe her interest in you as strictly maternal, Micki," Noelle said cynically.

"Noelle, we chatted last week, ran into each other by coincidence Wednesday night. She asked me if she and a friend could have a ride down, I had no reason to refuse, and that's all there is to it."

"You don't have to sound so defensive," Noelle replied.

Micki didn't respond to the comment; rather, she finished her coffee, told Noelle it had been a long day for her, and that they'd be sure to see each other again before the weekend was over.

CHAPTER 4

It was some time before Angela told Micki how she had spent the evening. Of course there was no friend from the city she had planned on meeting. Her only reason for the trip to P-town that weekend was to give her a chance to be with Micki again.

When Angela left Micki and Noelle, she moved quickly through the crowd and out onto the deck of the Blue Moon. She used the stairs leading to the beach for her exit, walked around to the front of the building, then waited for Micki to leave the club.

Micki soon strolled up the crushed gravel path. Angela stepped back into the shadows, watched Micki head for her car and drive up Commercial Street.

With no other plans for the evening, Angela decided to stop in at the Atlantic House on the chance that Gary might be there. She approached the doorman who began to shake his head, discouraging her from coming any further.

"Try the Blue Moon or the Pied Piper," he said in a pleasant voice. "There's no action for you here."

"I know *that*," she replied pertly. "I just want to peek in and see if a friend of mine is here. Do you mind?"

"Be my guest, darlin', go right ahead."

She stepped past the cigarette machine into the doorway that opened onto the Small Bar. The room was dark, sweaty, musky. Sad lyrics from an old Billie Holiday record could be heard over the low murmur of many conversations.

From behind the bar, a handsome, bearded man called, "What can I get you?"

"Nothing right now, thanks," Angela replied.

She scanned the room, but Gary was nowhere to be seen. She stepped outside, glanced at the men sitting on the porch of the A-House Hotel, and gave up on finding her friend.

Then, as if a fairy godmother had granted her wish, Gary skipped down the short flight of stairs leading from Bradford Street onto the short alley.

"Gary," she called out excitedly, "I've been looking for you."

"If you want some of my coke now, the answer is no. No. No. No. You had your chance a few hours ago, but I can't give you what I don't have any of, can I, Miss Angela?" His sentences ran together, phrases were delivered in a rapid-fire, high-pitched voice. "But excuse me, that delightful snowy substance is brand *new* to you, am I right?"

"What difference does it make?" Angela said sullenly. "I just need someone familiar to connect with. You must know what that feeling's like."

"Feeling spooked?"

"Not spooked."

"Then what, baby? Want to tell me over coffee?"

"No, I can see you're ready for play," she said, her voice depressed. "I'll head on back to the room."

They walked toward the street and suddenly Angela's mood changed.

"Wasn't it fun coming down with Micki?" she asked brightly. "What'd you think of her?"

"Sexy lady," Gary responded easily.

"Sexy lady? That's all?"

"Angela, you are as transparent as spun glass," he replied with a laugh. "Do you think I don't know what this is all about? The dinner the other evening, the ride down tonight? You are stalking your prey, aren't you?"

"What if I am? What *do* you think of her? *Really*?"

"I just don't get it," he said taking her hand.

"Get what?"

"What's the big attraction? You're riding the crest of a wave right now, you could have *anyone*. Walk into a woman's bar in this...or *any* town...and take your pick."

"And?"

"It won't be easy for you if you push this with her."

"What are you talking about?"

"*Complications*, baby," Gary said, draping his arm over her shoulder. "All right, the age difference, for one thing."

She shrugged, but other than that, didn't respond.

He hugged her, then spoke softly. "Angel, baby, we all pick our own merry-go-rounds. If you go for this gold ring, I just hope that before the ride's over, you're not sorry it hadn't been on another carousel."

"I'm going to have her, Gary."

"I know you are. Just try not to get hurt."

"I thought you'd be happy for me, see her the way I do, know how I feel--"

"Angela, *stop*! You're happy? I'm happy. Fair enough? Come on, let's walk down town for a coffee."

"No, I think I'll head back. You go have fun for the two of us."

"Sweet dreams, then love," he said and kissed her on the cheek.

*****

Angela was up and about early Saturday morning. She strolled to a nearby restaurant for breakfast, choosing a table outside in the sun for her morning juice and coffee.

The scene from the deck was pleasant: clear blue sky, a calm sea, sails drifting back and forth in the lazy morning breezes, occasional gulls flying overhead. Angela leaned back in her chair, lulled by the peacefulness of it all.

When she finished, she hopped a bus for Race Point. She'd decided it would be less crowded than Herring Cove, the gay beach near town, and she wanted this time alone.

Angela walked past the Coast Guard station and continued another quarter of a mile until she saw that she had the beach to herself.

She felt calm, in control of events. A feeling of assurance that all would work out as planned swept over her body, warmed her as much as the summer sun.

Next week, Angela thought, I'll invite her as my guest to the opening at the Museum. We'll meet for dinner before, some quiet Back Bay restaurant, and *I'll* choose the wine.

I don't want to rush things, though. I know she's holding back, otherwise she would have come to my room last week. I've got to try to imagine what her life must be like. She probably doesn't do much of *anything* on impulse and she must be a *fixture* at that department store by now. She's taken by me, though...that much I'm sure of.

Excited by the thoughts now running through her mind, Angela sat up. The surf was high, white caps broke on the beach, one string after another, like crystal shattering on the shore.

I can *feel* that we're right for each other, she told herself. She must feel it, too. Angela hugged her knees, watched the deep blue churning sea, assured herself again that she had every reason for the strong sense of confidence she felt.

She gazed admiringly at the full sails of a schooner, constructing an image of Micki as she watched the ship sail toward the horizon. Micki was secure, she decided. She liked that about her. She was honest, Angela reflected, and didn't hesitate to talk about her past, her marriage, her son. She was successful; her position at Hewitt's proved that. Physically, Micki was just right. Angela had long found blondes attractive...and her eyes, she recalled, had been so warm and accepting as she'd received Angela's watch.

By noon, Angela was ready to return to town. In buoyant spirits, she headed for the bus stop, wondering when she'd see Micki next.

Micki spent the morning taking in her favorite shops. She knew that many of the avant garde styles she saw in P-town would soon make their way to Boston. She wondered which of these styles would be appropriate for the rather conservative shoppers who frequented Hewitt's.

She stopped at an oyster bar and watched the dark, curly-haired shucker take his knife, slice across the shells and slip under the pearly-grey flesh. Six fresh oysters with a wedge of lemon and a paper cup of hot sauce were arranged on a plastic plate and passed to the next customer in line. She took a seat at the polished mahogany bar and with a plastic prong, speared a glistening oyster, dipped it in the sauce and brought it to her lips. She raised the shell to her mouth, drank the juice.

Pleased with the way the morning had passed, Micki stepped out into bright sunlight, crossed the street and decided to stop at a sidewalk cafe. It seemed a relaxing spot from which to watch tourists making their way down the always crowded Commercial Street. Micki sat comfortably under the shade of a leafy tree. She was enjoying her time alone. She'd thought of Angela often that morning as she continued to try to convince herself that even though she found her a most intriguing, most attractive young woman, at this point in her life, she didn't want complications.

She'd worked hard at dealing with the pain of a marriage which had ended, with the bitter custody battle that she had lost, with the estrangement from her son Mark, who was now already in graduate school. Obligatory calls over the holidays, a post card now and then from his travels, occasionally a photo, she mused, that's all she had of Mark. That was all, she concluded, she could expect.

She didn't know how she ever made it through those first months without him, those early years alone, calling Mark in the L.A. suburb Guy had moved to after the divorce, hearing the small voice answer in angry monosyllables when she asked him how he liked his new school or his new house, promising him she would try to bring him back to Boston for the whole summer, not just a two-week vacation, then adjusting to the coolness of his voice as he gradually lost interest in asking if he could "come home," as he gradually adjusted.

Now, for Micki, being alone was her comfort. She couldn't stand the threat of another loss, which, she told herself, could occur for almost any reason if she allowed herself to be vulnerable once more, open to a new relationship. She had barely kept her head together during the divorce and the bleak months which had followed. Noelle had helped some, but no one could have given her what she needed then. What she needed was the love of her child. She reflected on how quickly the years had passed; now Mark was a man himself. Childhood was no more than a memory for both of them.

Micki had finally come to feel secure about herself, and she wanted to hold on to just what she had that afternoon--the time to be free for days just such as this. She leaned back in the chair, closed her eyes for a moment until she heard the voice of a young woman asking her if she'd had enough time to see the menu.

Micki looked up, smiled, and ordered a cappucino.

Later that afternoon, she stopped in at the Blue Moon. She was surprised to see that except for Jessie and Noelle at the piano and Lana behind the bar, the club was deserted.

"Must be a great day at the beach," Micki called out in a friendly voice.

"You want sun, pretty lady? Sit on the deck. Those two are hard at work from what I can tell. Awfully pretty music coming out of that piano today."

"I'll just sit and listen," she replied.

She ordered a tall tonic water and sat patiently as they worked over some phrases from what must have been a new song. Jessie tried the lyrics of the beginning one more time and when she finished, Micki applauded.

"You like it?" she asked.

"It's lovely, Jessie, I mean it."

"It's not quite right yet, though, is it, Noelle?"

"You're the perfectionist, Jessie; you'll know when it's ready."

"I think we can put it away for today," Jessie replied. "Besides, I want to get ready for the party. Going to join us, Micki?"

"Yes, do," Noelle encouraged her. "It's the Boatslip's annual costume tea dance."

"A *big* event, I can tell," Micki said ironically. "How could I possibly miss it?"

"We'll meet around four, all right?"

"Will I recognize you?" she asked.

"Sure," Noelle replied, "look for the blond wig. I'm coming as Madonna."

They were all in the mood for a good time, especially since Jessie had arranged to have a friend work the early part of the afternoon for her. None of them wore costumes, though. They'd decided to leave that to more fanciful personalities.

They headed for the pool, where bathing beauties of both sexes took in the late afternoon sun. Standing in a circle near the bar were six beautiful black drag queens, not one under six three or over a hundred and forty pounds.

"How do they do it, Micki?" Noelle asked with a certain amount of admiration. "What do you think, Jessie? Low fat diets? Natural foods?"

"More likely a natural substance known as cocaine," Micki said as she glanced in their direction. "Whatever it is, I'll agree that they're stunning."

Dressed in suits of gold and silver lamé and shoulder length marcelled hairdos, wigs fashioned in the forties style, they pranced on spike heels, weaving to the beat of the music.

"The time and money these girls spend on makeup must be something else," Micki said, laughing lightly.

"They're so *pretty*," Jessie replied. "I'm jealous!"

Then Micki heard a familiar voice from behind.

"Jessie...Noelle... Micki," Angela cooed as she put a friendly arm around Micki and Noelle's waists. "Imagine seeing you here."

"Angela," Jessie responded in a friendly tone, "you *did* come back. I thought you were just making polite conversation last week."

"No, I meant what I said. I plan to do the story I mentioned, too."

Micki observed their animated conversation. "This is a *small* world," she said finally. "I didn't know you two knew each other."

"Who, Jessie and me?" Angela asked innocently. "We're chums from way back, aren't we, hon?"

Jessie twirled her red hair in her fingers, smiled at Noelle and said, "Feel like dancing?"

They walked toward the dance floor, and Angela turned to Micki. "How about it, driver," she asked, "in the mood for another dance?"

There was such seduction in her tone that Micki didn't know how...or why...she refused, but she did.

Angela was undaunted. She told Micki that her friend Gary had decided to stay on for a few more days. It would be just the two of them going back to Boston.

Obviously disappointed in Micki's lack of reaction, she said, "I don't know why, Micki, but I just don't think you're happy to see me."

"I'm happy to see *everyone*, Angela," Micki responded. Angela stepped closer to Micki. "You don't seem to be having a good weekend; you're tense. I told you, you and I can leave *early*."

"No change in plans, Angela," Micki said firmly, "Sunday night at seven, all right?"

"Yes *ma'am*," Angela replied. "Can't I at least buy you a drink? What shall it be? A round of Perrier's? From the looks of people arriving, this party's just getting started."

Micki shrugged her shoulders and Angela looked out over the crowded dance floor to the sea and the sky beyond. Though they were standing next to each other, she and Micki seemed miles apart.

Micki excused herself to visit the john, and as Angela watched her walk across the room, she decided to follow. When she opened the door, Micki was standing in front of a mirror combing her hair.

"Hi, Micki," she said softly.

"Hello, Angela," Micki replied. "What's wrong? Not enough action on the dance floor?"

"You're so short with me, Micki. Why? I don't get it. We had such a good time driving down last night, didn't we?"

Micki turned to face Angela. "Yes...and I'm sorry. For some reason, I'm just not in the mood for a party."

"Is it anything I'm doing? Am I bothering you?"

"Angela, I don't want things to get out of hand."

"Like last week, you mean?"

Micki nodded.

"Okay, Micki, I hear you."

"I think you do...I'm glad."

"Are you?"

"Yes," Micki replied.

"Then let's kiss and make up."

"You see, that's what I mean," Micki said gently.

"Can't we be friends?" Angela asked, an innocent smile in her eyes.

"Of course we can," Micki said, as Angela stepped closer to kiss her lightly on the lips.

Micki pulled back at first, then pressed forward to meet Angela's lips. She held Angela in her arms and whispered, "It just won't work. Can't you take my word for it?"

Angela traced Micki's mouth with her thumb, teasing Micki's lips.

"I know you want me," Angela said insistently. "Every bit as much as I want you."

Angela touched Micki's breasts and bent her head to kiss them through the light fabric of her shirt.

"The door's going to open any minute," Micki said in protest.

"Let it."

Deftly, she unbuttoned the shirt and bent to kiss the full softness. Micki pulled Angela up and covered herself, quickly buttoning her shirt. Angela said nothing but pressed her lips to Micki's once again.

Micki returned the kiss with passion, held Angela's face between her two hands, shook her own head no.

But Angela pulled Micki to her and their lips met once again. Angela murmured soft sounds of love, played teasingly with Micki's tongue, invited her to other passions.

"Let's leave, let's just go," Angela whispered urgently. "Anywhere."

Micki brought Angela's hands to her face and kissed her fingertips.

"Nowhere," Micki said softly. "Nowhere, Angela." She reached for Angela and held her in her arms as if she were a child. "Let's go back to the others."

"Why?"

"We have to. I mean what I'm saying." Tenderly, she brushed Angela's hair back from her forehead.

"You could love me," Angela said quietly.

"I know."

"Who's keeping us apart? Is there someone else?" she asked urgently.

"No."

"I don't believe you. Who is it?"

"It's me, Angela," Micki said with a slight, sad smile. "Just me."

"I don't know what you're talking about," she protested, placing her hands firmly on Micki's shoulders.

"It's hard to explain...I don't feel ready for a relationship. Maybe this is all happening too fast, maybe I've been alone too long, but Angela, you have to hear what I'm saying."

But the angry expression in Angela's eyes revealed that she wasn't listening. As the door swung open, Angela broke away and brushed past three young women who were walking in. Micki let her go.

When Angela eventually got around to telling Micki about her response to what she described as "the first brush-off" of her life, she didn't spare any of the details.

She said she felt frantic when she left the bar, angry at herself because she'd spent a good part of that day planning each step of what she felt was sure to be the direction their relationship would take. She'd spun fantasies of candlelight dinners, theater openings, intimate evenings...and what had she done? Tried to force herself on Micki.

And where? It couldn't have been a more dismal scenario, she lamented.

From the bar, she returned to her room, rummaged through bags for her supply of uppers and downers. She grabbed two pills, swallowed them, stuffed the bottle back in her purse, tossed the purse across the room.

She paced the room, back and forth, from the window to the door and back again. She kicked her suitcase across the floor, threw herself into a chair, clenched her fists and held her arms tight against her body.

Who does she think she *is*, she asked herself, treating me like that? Doesn't she know who I am? Doesn't she KNOW? She thinks she can throw me over? She's dreaming. That lady's *dreaming*!

She tried the door to Gary's room and found it was unlocked. She knew she'd find a bit of what she was after; she was sure he'd never leave himself without a treat. She located the small aluminum packet at the bottom of his shaving kit. When she saw the crushed white grains of cocaine, she decided there was plenty for the two of them.

Back in her room, she sang to herself as she cut the grains, arranging them in four narrow lines. She took a crisp dollar bill from her wallet, rolled it back and forth in her palms until it formed a narrow cylinder. Then she bent over the small mirror, inserted the cylinder in her right nostril, held her left nostril shut with her index finger, and inhaled.

She snorted again, deeply, breathing in pleasure that she knew would momentarily be hers. Just as she felt the drip of mucous in her throat, she bent her head over the mirror again, this time holding her right nostril shut and inhaling with her left. Then she closed her eyes and let her head fall back on the chair.

"Thank you, Gary," she said out loud, opening her eyes to look around the room. She inhaled deeply again, drawing whatever cocaine and mucous that might be left in her nostrils down into her throat.

She stood in front of the mirrored dresser, running her hands down the length of her body as she admired herself.

"Hey, Micki," she said, "you should be here with me now. I'd show you a good time, that's for sure."

Angela laughed and pirouetted before the mirror.

"Why, you're beautiful, Angela, so *beautiful.*"

She smiled at herself, leaned close to the mirror and kissed the woman in the glass. She unbuttoned the silk shirt she wore, stepped out of her slacks and admired the image of herself in lace bra and satin briefs.

"What do you say, Micki? Would you like to see this?"

She turned and faced the chair, posing as if Micki did, indeed, sit before her. She reached behind her back and unsnapped her bra, throwing it at the chair. She cupped her breasts, thrust her pelvis forward, moved her body slowly to music she heard somewhere in her head.

"Like it?" she asked. "In the mood for more?"

She stepped out of her pants and dangled the white briefs on the tip of her toe.

"You couldn't get this twice in one lifetime, Micki, so who you kidding? Huh? *Who*?"

She turned to face herself in the mirror. She laughed as she struck one of her usual on-camera poses.

"This is all a goddamn nasty joke, isn't it?" she asked.

And then almost as quickly as she'd gone up, she came down, gazing at reflections of herself, reaching out for whirling images that stared back at her from the mirror. She saw secrets of sorrow: her dead mother's sweet face, love that came to her only in her dreams, loneliness that she'd not shared with anyone, hunger she thought she'd forgotten. They were all too much for her, and she quickly turned away from memories of the child whose dark eyes held her past. When she looked into the mirror again, she saw how sleek she was, how tanned, her hair a chic circle of curls, brushed forward. She smiled in approval, though tears she'd held back still glistened in her eyes, reflecting harsh light from the inexpensive lamp that shone on the mirror she viewed.

She picked up her brush, ran it through her hair roughly, once, twice, three times, stiff bristles stinging her scalp. She continued brushing, detaching herself from the past, as pain pulled her into the present, into the now.

"Hey, baby, do you like what you *see*?" she asked, a sudden surge coursing through her body. "Well, you're going to, Micki...I just need a little more time to show you what I'm all about. You'll learn, darling...I've got a hundred and twenty six miles between here and Boston to teach you."

CHAPTER 5

When Noelle reminded Jessie that it was time to leave the Boatslip for her stint at the Blue Moon snack bar, Micki suggested that they stroll back with her and then walk on into town.

They passed a row of shops crowded with tourists, and Noelle noticed that Micki seemed quiet, preoccupied.

"Something's troubling you, isn't it?" she asked, putting an arm around Micki's shoulder, giving her a hug. "Or is it *someone*?"

"I'm sure you know who it is," Micki replied thoughtfully. The perplexed expression on her face conveyed the dilemma. "Angela attracts me, that's for sure," Micki continued, "but she also terrifies me. She's incredibly...needy."

"And other people aren't?" Noelle inquired.

"I don't think so," Micki answered. "At least not from my own experience."

"Guy wasn't needy?" Noelle asked candidly.

"Oh, yes," Micki agreed, "in his own insidious way, he most certainly was. He was *so* happy when I got the job at Hewitt's. All of his worries about how he'd be supported while he went on to law school just disappeared.

"Back then, I had my own thoughts about grad school, but Hewitt's spelled security...at least that's what Guy told me.

"I applied to Boston University's broadcast journalism program, even managed to take a few night courses. But my schedule at the store was so erratic then. That was a long time ago," she said, "why am I talking about it now?"

"Angela, remember?" Noelle said lightly.

"Right. I wonder if part of my attraction is because she's succeeding in a profession I once wanted for myself," Micki said, struggling for answers.

"I don't want you to think I'm dissatisfied, Noelle," she continued, "I've done well in retailing. After all, not all buyers end up as division heads."

She shook her head, wanting to wash away a flood of memories that surfaced. From the beginning, Guy had wanted to work in corporate law. The law firm demanded long hours, considerable travel, but weekends, he'd said, were for relaxation. For Guy, this meant drinking, and soon weekends began with cocktails, ended with nightcaps. There was nothing in between. Their marriage became a blur of mutual avoidances, Micki recalled. She learned of Guy's infidelities, first in Boston and later while he was traveling.

Mark was their only common focus. Then with the divorce, Guy's accusations, the legal expertise at his fingertips, she lost her son. She was granted a generous financial settlement, the Beacon Street condo, and the Mercedes she still drove, but that could never replace the loss of her child.

"Angela's stirring up so many deep feelings in you, Micki," Noelle said, drawing Micki from her thoughts.

"You're right about that," she replied. "Why don't I try to put it all on hold for now. Let's enjoy the walk."

Micki smiled at Noelle as they observed straight couples meandering by, walking hand in hand, as if they were clasping each other for security.

"Think some of these folks wish they'd spent the day in Hyannis?" Noelle said lightly, conceding to Micki's wish to change the subject.

Micki laughed. "Probably," she said. "It's as if they're wearing blinders, isn't it?"

Life in Provincetown is a kaleidoscope of many shapes and colors, Micki mused, enjoying the crush of tourists on the crowded street.

Summer was ripening slowly in Provincetown that year. There was still a sense of expectation in the shops and clubs, a feeling that the season, although it had made its traditional entrance over Memorial Day a few weeks ago, hadn't quite begun. As usual, June was a cool month on the Cape and perhaps those who were exploring its shores at this time of year were as tentative about the season as the climate itself. It had rained much of the month, day after day, through the nights, on into the afternoons, and the cloud cover that had drifted in over the upper Cape that afternoon was one of the reasons there was so much street traffic at this time of the day.

Tourists watched their wallets in June, though, browsing and window shopping, rather than buying. No doubt they were saving summer's abandon for late July and August. Now they were content to meander slowly down this main street that's like no other in the land.

Approaching the Pinocchio Shop, they decided to stop in to say hello to Phyllis, a mutual friend of many years. She was just about to display her latest creation in the front window--a plump puppet dressed in braid-trimmed velvet.

"How do you like Reginald?" she asked. "I finished the last stitch on his jacket only ten minutes ago."

"Handsome," Noelle said. "A charmer."

"Hope customers feel the same way," she replied, a broad smile on her freckled face.

"Sales off?" Micki asked, looking about the shop.

"A bit, but a few good weekends will make up for it."

They all agreed, knowing the cycle of summer trade in P-town's many shops. In Provincetown, where more people than not were still children at heart, her toy shop was a great success. Winters Phyllis stayed snug in a small village near Hartford, making puppets, dolls, games. Early each spring, she packed her van, closed her house and headed for the Cape. She'd made a second home for herself in Pinocchio's and her shop was a charming place.

"I've missed seeing you at the Club," Noelle said.

"I'll be down one of these nights; you know I always make an appearance or two."

Phil had lived alone these past seven years, winter and summer, since Ceil, her lover of many years, had been killed in an automobile accident. It would seem that the passing years would have eased her grief, but for whatever her reasons, she'd not become involved in another relationship. Her shop, her craft, her friends seemed to contribute to her own strong sense of self-sufficiency.

"Don't wait till Labor Day weekend," Noelle warned.

"I won't," she said chuckling. "It's always such fun to see the baby dykes on parade."

"Compared to us," Noelle replied, "they're all babes!"

Though she and Phyllis laughingly agreed to this, Micki didn't respond. She walked over to one of the toy displays, picked up a graceful ballerina puppet and tried to manipulate the strings, while Noelle and Phyllis caught up on the odds and ends of the past winter. Soon customers crossing the threshold of the shop called Phyllis back to work.

Outside once more, Micki asked, "Feel like stopping off at the Town House to say hello to Annie?"

Noelle shook her head. "I still need to take care of a few things for tonight's show. Will you be dropping by?"

"If I don't," Micki said, "we've still all got our date for the beach tomorrow."

"For sure," Noelle answered.

Micki leaned forward, kissed her lightly on the cheek. "Thanks for being such a good listener."

The Town House had long been the gathering spot for those who'd been around as early as the fifties, and if the crowd seemed to grow older each year, which it did, spirits remained as young as ever. The sing-along was the usual attraction, as songs popular in decades past were harmonized by the motley crew, which now and then encouraged one of its own to stand by the piano, to lead the group, to indulge in a boozy bit of show-biz. Micki felt she could use the sight of the friendly faces she was bound to find there.

By morning, the thick cloud cover that had blown in the day before had been swept out to sea. When Noelle and Jessie arrived at Herring Cove Beach, the sun on their bodies felt as hot and fresh as clean towels. The sky was bright blue, clear as a freshly painted watercolor. Curly white clouds, lambs' tails, were scattered across the heavens. Swift winds blew them westward.

They ambled down toward the women's section and when they saw Micki waving to them, headed for the spot she'd picked out. They dropped their beach gear and blanket on the sand, unpacked towels, lotion, sun visors.

"We didn't see you last night," Noelle teased. "Find an interesting diversion for yourself?"

"Not at all," Micki replied. "I picked up the papers, a few magazines and turned in early."

As Jessie and Noelle stripped to their suits, Micki, who wore red jogging shorts and a sleeveless T-shirt, raised the shirt over her head and pulled it off. Noticing the bit of a stir she was causing sans suit, she stood, surveyed the scene around her, looked out, checked the tide and then lazily lay back down on the blanket.

"Having fun?" Noelle inquired.

She laughed. "You know what they say...if you've got it flaunt it."

"They *still* say that?" Noelle replied.

"Back in Boston they do," she said saucily. "Before you get settled, Noelle, would you rub a little sun screen on my back? The sun is *hot!*"

"Sure," Noelle obliged.

Noelle leaned over, uncapped the tube, squeezed. She traced the letter Z on Micki's back, massaging her shoulders.

"Very nice, Noelle, take your time. Jessie," she called over, "I hope you appreciate all the talents this woman has."

"Each and every one," Jessie said, savoring the words.

"You better," Noelle said insistently, as she dropped the sun screen on Micki's towel and moved closer to Jessie.

"This is pure bliss," Micki sighed. "What peace, absolute heaven."

"Why bless my britches," a loud voice called from a nearby dune, "it's three of my favorite pretty ladies."

"I knew I wasn't destined to last long in heaven," Micki groaned.

As Noelle sat up to greet Lana and Ruth, she slapped Micki's shoulders in a playful reprimand.

"Hey, Lana," Micki asked in a friendly voice, "what's cooking?"

"Cooking? Nothing. We just brought some sandwiches and iced tea."

Micki smiled at Lana's reply as she took in Lana's beach attire. "That's some outfit, Lana," she responded.

Lana smiled in agreement, her eyes and face shaded from the sun by an over-sized plastic visored straw hat. She wore a bright Hawaiian print shirt, khaki walking shorts, black, high-top sneakers and lavender socks. Ruth, clutching a wicker straw lunch basket in her two hands, was dressed more simply in a navy sun dress and sandals.

"Out for a swim?" Noelle asked.

"For sure," Lana replied. "My best girl and I are enjoying every moment of this weekend."

She squatted in the sand, leaned back on her haunches. "When Ruthie and I first got together ten years ago, we had more than our share of...sexual problems. Just couldn't work them out. We're more mature now, thank goodness, and we're giving things another try. Ruthie's brought some great toys with her. Know what I mean, ladies?"

She stood, shoved her hands in her shorts pockets and laughed. Ruth, her face scarlet, looked as if she wanted to bury her head in the sand.

"Hon, let's tell them about our favorite. We had more *fun* with it!" Lana wrapped a large arm around Ruth's shoulders, pulled her close.

"Lana, that's just for us," Ruth whispered angrily.

"What?" Lana asked, looking down at her with concern. "Oh, right, got you. It's private, ladies, know what I mean?"

"You and Jessie want some sun screen, Noelle?" Micki asked, changing the subject.

"Sure," she said, sitting up, as anxious as Micki was to veer the subject from Ruth and Lana's sex life.

Micki tossed the tube of lotion to Jessie. "Looks to me as if you're both getting awfully red," she cautioned.

As Noelle propped herself up on her elbows and waited for Jessie to apply the sunscreen, she noticed Lana and Ruth taking in the scene with discomfort. She glanced over and saw that Micki was the source of embarrassment for them.

"The rangers don't go for that sort of thing," Lana said sternly.

"What rangers?" Micki asked innocently.

"The *rangers*," Lana repeated. "This is part of the National Sea Shore. They patrol. On horseback. You have to be covered."

"Let 'em catch me first," Micki said, standing up to survey the scene. More women than not were topless so Micki shrugged. "Why the fuss, Lana?"

"Ruthie," she said intensely, "look at the boats out there."

"Pretty," Ruth replied, paying her no attention.

"Micki, where *are* your manners?" Lana asked. "You're embarrassing Ruth, we're going to have to sit somewhere else."

"Why?" Micki asked.

"Stop staring, Ruth, turn your head the other way. Watch the *sail boats!*" Though Lana was insistent, there seemed to be no way to divert Ruth's attention. "So, Ruth, you *haven't* changed," she exploded. "You're still a peeper! A voyeur! Let these fools wait for the rangers to make their arrests, I'm putting you on the first bus out of town.

"Nice going, Noelle," she scolded. "How you going to like singing your pretty tunes from a jail cell?"

At that, Micki, Noelle and even Jessie burst into laughter as Lana reached for Ruth's arm and pulled her away.

"Let's go," Lana said angrily. "I want to check the bus schedule back to the Big Apple."

"But Lana," Ruth protested, "what about our dune buggy ride? What about our plans for August?"

"I've got a migraine coming on," Lana retorted, "I want to get back to town before it hits."

"I've got aspirin with me--"

"Aspirin," Lana snorted. "As if aspirin would help. And when you pack, don't forget to take your...toys!"

"Lana, we were just getting started again, we've had such a good time. And I *can't* go back on the bus. It was so crowded coming up, I thought I'd faint. You know I can't take crowds for long periods of time."

"And to you people this is *funny*," Lana said accusingly.

"Ah, no," Noelle began, "don't be upset, Lana."

"How can I not be? I've got a migraine, and Ruthie's agoraphobia is back! Micki, you're giving a bad name to those of us who respect modesty...privacy...the way Ruthie and I do."

"Do I really have to go back, Lana? I just got here."

"Oh, hell, no," she said wearily. "Let's just go down by the water and eat our sandwiches."

"Stay," Micki urged. "I'll even put my shirt back on."

"Never mind," Lana sputtered. "We're going to enjoy the scenery. Come on, Ruthie, it's still a nice day for us."

"Lana," Noelle called out, "we'll see you later at the Blue Moon."

"If the whole bunch of you aren't hauled off to jail first," she replied. "And Micki, you *should* cover yourself. I'd never make a public display of *my* body."

"I will, Lana," Micki said agreeably.

As the two women walked toward the water, Noelle said, "That wasn't very nice, was it?"

"No," Jessie replied, "it wasn't, but we're alone again and I guess that's what you two wanted."

"It is more peaceful without Lana, don't you agree?" Micki asked.

Noelle and Jessie nodded. It was.

A few minutes later, Noelle felt herself dozing off, as she enjoyed the warmth from the sun and the soft, lovely music played by a young woman a few blankets away. The melody being played on the guitar was a comforting contrast to the loud beat from boom-boxes usually heard at the beach.

It was a lazy afternoon for them all. Jessie and Micki walked down to the shore to see the progress two women were making on their wind surfers. Noelle soon joined them and then decided that if she was going to take a swim it had better be soon. She had a matinee at the Club that afternoon, and Jessie would need to get back soon as well.

It was high tide. Rather than prolong the agonizing chill of the water and wade in, she dove into the surf, turned on her back, floated out to sea and waited for the next run of waves. It didn't take her in very far, and she began a back stroke that took her fifty feet or so out into the water. Then she turned over on her stomach, executed a half dozen or so breast strokes until she met the next wave. To her surprise, Micki bobbed up a few feet away, shaking salt water from her hair.

"Where's Jessie?" Noelle inquired.

"She's gone after Lana and Ruth."

Noelle looked toward the shore and spotted Jessie's red hair and dark green one piece bathing suit. Some distance beyond, she saw two figures that must be Lana and Ruth. They were strolling hand in hand toward a sand bar.

In the early afternoon sun, the water was a deep, inky blue. Beyond the beach, lush red pasture roses grew along the stretch of grass covered dunes.

"One more wave and I'll head on in," Noelle called as the swells mounted behind her. She took a deep breath, put her face in the water, stretched out her arms and floated in to shore. It was just like going home, she reflected.

Micki was close behind. Noelle waited for her.

"It's been one perfect day, hasn't it?" Noelle asked.

"It reminds me of all the things I liked best when I was a kid," Micki said, her tone suggesting reminiscence.

"What were they? What did you especially like?" she inquired.

"Oh...summer showers." Micki smiled as she recalled the past. "Late afternoon summer showers. My mother used to let me go out into the back yard to run through the rain. One day I got the idea that it would be fun to take my clothes off, and when I did, she just stood and watched me play.

"Another time, the kids next door were over and we all ran starkers through the rain. Life was simple then...and sweet.

"I can still see my mother looking out from the back porch...smiling at us all running through the rain."

There was a tinge of sadness in her voice that was rarely present when Micki spoke.

"It's a lovely memory, Micki," Noelle replied. "What brings it to mind?"

"How quickly it all slips by, I suppose, how fast time passes. My mother's gone now, my father, too. Now there's only my sister, Kathleen. And we don't see each other very often," she said regretfully.

"She's still living in the same small town south of Pittsburgh...where life seemed to be so simple to me. I know it's not possible, but I still want my life to be that way, Noelle. Simple...without complications. Is that selfish?"

"Not necessarily," Noelle answered. "Is that what's troubling you? Complications?"

"No," she said insistently. "Now and then I just need to be able to say to someone what *does* matter to me."

Changing the subject, she gestured to Jessie, Lana and Ruth out on the sand bar. "What are they *doing* out there?"

"Gathering beach stones," Noelle suggested. "They'll be back soon."

"I hope so, I'd like to say goodbye before I set out for the city."

"Why not stay with us tonight? Get up early tomorrow and drive on in then."

She shook her head. "I need to get back tonight. Besides, I've got a passenger going back with me."

"Angela?" Noelle asked.

"Yes. If she remembers to meet me."

Noelle looked at Micki quizzically. "You don't really think she'll forget, do you?" she asked.

CHAPTER 6

As good as her word, Micki was right on time that evening. Angela hopped down from the porch of her guest house, crossed in front of the car and climbed in.

"Your friend hasn't changed his mind about heading back with us?" Micki asked.

"Gary? Afraid not. Something pretty exciting must have come up for him last night."

"And how about you? Close up the bars?"

"No, I went to a party out on Shank Painter Road. At Trish Wilson's place. Know her by any chance?"

"Should I?"

"She's a New York architect, seems to know everyone. Don't you get down to the city fairly often?"

"Yes, but on business."

"You never mix in a little pleasure?" Angela asked mischievously.

Micki gave a noncommittal shrug and turned her attention to the road.

"You should have seen her place, Micki. Back off the road, hidden by the trees, walls that seemed to be made of nothing but glass and polished oak. *Very* dramatic. And you?"

"Last night? Nothing much," Micki replied truthfully, "I turned in early."

"Is that so?"

Angela looked out of the window and thought of how she *had* spent last night...not at a party on Shank Painter Road, but in her room...alone.

When she'd come down from her cocaine high, she'd sat naked, shivering in the night air, until she realized that all she wanted to do was to get under the covers and sleep. She wanted to block out everything. Everyone. Except Micki.

Micki drove along Route 6A until they passed through Truro. The first of the summer moons was full, and floated like a pale disc high in the clear blue early evening sky. "Pretty, isn't it?" she asked.

"I'd never take you for a star gazer, Micki. I'm going to learn all kinds of interesting things about you."

"I'll learn a few about you, too," she said pleasantly.

"Let me make it real easy for you," Angela answered directly, turning to face her. "What would you like to know?"

"Whatever you'd supply for an interview."

"Photos, too?" she teased.

"You have them with you?"

They laughed and Angela shook her head no.

"It's still a hike to Boston," she said, "but I promise to invite you up to see my complete portfolio. In living color. Actually, I've quite a collection. I was involved with a photographer last summer who never stopped snapping."

"Why aren't you still together?" Micki asked gently.

"Who knows? She was more interested in taking *pictures* of me than *me*, if you can figure that one out. Whatever, it was no big deal. We had an easy, casual parting of the ways. That's my style, Micki. Love 'em and leave 'em *easy*. No hard feelings that way."

"Have you had many lovers?"

"Me? Moi? Why? Do I look it?"

"I doubt you've spent the last few years in meditation."

"No, we're activists in my family. There's too much going on in the world for meditation. Last week you told me about your interest in politics, your involvement with the struggle for civil rights. Well, I have political allegiances, too, though they're different from yours. Remember the Bay of Pigs? My father took part in that. He was one

59

of the heroes who survived President Kennedy's botched attempt to generate Cuban support against Castro. He'd only been in Miami a few months when he joined friends of his who had been persuaded by the CIA's promises of an overthrow in Cuba. He told me once that they were all killed, his friends. He felt betrayed, bitter, but grateful that he was able to come back to the States. He's not bitter about it any more, though he still lives in Miami, still dreams of a time when Cuba will be free. He's not alone; the movement continues to grow. I think one day it will happen," she said passionately.

"And your mother?" Micki asked, absorbing Angela's latest revelation.

Angela turned to gaze at the blur of scrub pines growing alongside the highway.

"I never knew her," Angela said sadly.

"Why?" Micki asked. "What happened?"

"She and my dad met just a few weeks after he arrived in Miami. It didn't take them long to fall in love, to marry. I was born the next year..." Angela's voice trailed off into silence.

"And?" Micki asked gently.

"Then my sister was born, Teresa, and finally, when I was three, Thomas, my brother."

"Then you did know her...your mother...didn't you?"

"I have memories, her face, her hair curling about her shoulders, her *smell*, so good to me, lipstick, perfume, coffee, her laugh...but especially, her eyes."

Angela was silent once more, finally she spoke, "She died before I was four...an accident...crossing the boulevard near our apartment. Hit and run my father was told, no clues then, but later, after the funeral, someone spoke to the police. Someone had seen the car speed off. The man was found, convicted, sent to jail. But what did that matter? He had left my mother at the side of the road, and she died on the way to the hospital."

"I'm sorry, Angela," Micki said compassionately.

Angela picked at loose threads on the sleeve of her jersey as she continued her story. "At first, my dad didn't have the strength to keep us all together. He thought we'd be better off with some of my mother's family, but then they couldn't keep us, and we were placed in foster homes--my sister and I with one family, my brother with another. All that I remember about that year is waiting for someone to come and get us. I wanted that someone to be my mother, but, of course, it never happened.

"Papa eventually put the pieces of his life back together and when he found a job as a super in an apartment complex that provided him with a large enough apartment, he rounded us all up and took us home." She laughed gently.

"It wasn't easy for him, Micki, and not everything turned out the way it does in story books. But I guess he did his best. Teresa finished law school this year and my brother is a teacher. Elementary school; he loves it."

"And you haven't done badly either, have you?" Micki replied with gentle encouragement. She reached out, squeezed Angela's hand.

"No, my Communications internship at the University of Florida led to an offer from a local TV station," Angela replied, intertwining her fingers with Micki's. "I worked there for nearly four years, then two years ago I was offered the job I now have at Channel 8. When I think of it, I know I've been terribly lucky."

"Luck's important, that's for sure," Micki answered, "but success demands much more than that. Give yourself the credit you deserve."

As they approached Wellfleet, Micki noticed bumper to bumper traffic down Route 6 for as far as she could see.

"Always a tie-up," she groaned. "Roads are widened everywhere else in the state, why not here?"

"Sounds like a lead for a story," Angela said lightly. "Say, would you believe I'm still in my bathing suit?"

"That can't be very comfortable. How come?"

"I wanted to catch some late afternoon sun after I'd checked out of my room. It's really sticking to all the wrong places right now."

"Let me stop at that restaurant up ahead. I could use a coffee and you can change there."

"Don't bother on my account," she said as she slipped out of her shorts and pulled her jersey over her head. Quickly, she slipped the straps of her bathing suit down over her shoulder and breasts, lifted her bottom and eased the suit down over her thighs and legs.

"There, that's better," Angela said, smiling at Micki. "You don't happen to have a towel handy, do you? I'd just like to brush off some sand."

"Couldn't you have waited until I stopped?" Micki's voice revealed irritation at what she saw as Angela's latest stunt.

"Why waste time? What's wrong? Am I embarrassing you?" she asked playfully.

"In case you haven't heard, Angela, P-town's the only liberal town on the Cape, and I doubt that even there you'd get away with a display like that if one of the boys with a badge happened to spot you."

"I only asked for a towel, Micki, not a lecture. I intend to get dressed, just let me brush off the sand."

Micki's eyes roamed the length of Angela's body. Olive colored skin, rich and inviting, small, rounded breasts, dark nipples, long, slender legs.

"Want to go parking?" she asked flirtatiously.

"Yes," Micki said quickly, lightly touching Angela's leg. "But we're not going to."

"I won't get dressed unless we do," Angela teased as she gripped Micki's wrist. "Buyer Blackmailed on Cape Cod Highway. I can see the headlines now."

Micki slapped her thigh playfully. "Come on, Angela, *get dressed!*" Micki was embarrassed that she couldn't quite handle the situation that was developing.

"If you insist," Angela said, reaching for her shorts and top.

The rest of the way back, Micki fought to distance herself from the image of Angela sitting next to her, flirting with her as she waved her jersey in the air like a flag. At the moment, Micki saw that she had only two choices; to pull into the next motel for the night, or to get back to Boston as soon as possible and to drop Angela at her doorstep.

Angela's moods had gone up and down a dozen times since they'd pulled out of P-town. She was talkative, wound-up, hyper one minute; dark, brooding, moody the next. And her pleading sensuality was very hard for Micki to resist.

Once again Micki saw her sitting naked beside her in the car. Some nerve...some body...D'Allessandro, she told herself, you better make your mind up. It's not every day that someone like Angela Hall is going to walk into your life.

What *would* she be like as a lover? She's one hell of a tease, that's for sure.

Why make such a production out of it? Why *not* take her home for the night? She's young, but not exactly a baby. Why am I resisting?

Micki continued the drive up the Cape Cod highway toward the Sagamore Bridge. She finally decided it would be best if the evening ended with them going their separate ways.

Though Angela's bright and animated conversation continued for most of the trip, as they approached Plymouth, she lapsed into a pensive mood.

"Falling asleep?" Micki asked.

"No, just thinking."

"About what?"

"Nothing much."

"This last stretch is tiring. We should have stopped for coffee along the way."

"I'll make you some at my place, how's that sound?" Angela asked quietly.

Micki paused before speaking, remembering the decision she'd made a short while ago. "Let's see how long it takes to drive these last fifty miles. There might be heavy traffic up ahead."

Angela shrugged. "You could still use a cup of coffee."

An hour later, merging with city-bound traffic on the expressway, Micki said, "Berkeley Street exit, right?"

"Mass. Ave. gets you off the expressway sooner."

"Right," Micki said, aware of a growing tension between them.

Angela directed her to West Newton Street and as luck would have it, there was a parking space across the street from her building.

"So how about some coffee?" Angela asked.

Micki pulled into the parking spot, cut the ignition, turned to face Angela.

"I want to try to get something straight with you, Angela. We both know what's going on between us; I'm not going to kid you about that. In as many different ways as I can, I've tried to let you know how I feel about it--"

"Even when I was changing my bathing suit, Micki?"

"Angela, stop it, I'm not playing with you, I want you to understand what I'm saying. We're at two very different places in life, that's clear, isn't it?"

"And *that's* the only reason you're holding back?"

Micki paused, leaned back in the seat, shook her head. "No," she said deliberately. "There's something about *you* that's troubling. Now maybe it's only in relation to me, so don't misunderstand--"

"What *is* it?" Angela asked anxiously.

"It's a quality I can't yet describe, but let me try. It has something to do with how you go after and probably get whatever you want...whatever you feel you *need*...without understanding *why* you need it."

"Shucks, ma'am," Angela scoffed, "I thought you didn't approve of my hairdo--"

"You wanted an answer," Micki said sharply, "I'm giving it to you as best as I can."

"I'm sorry, go ahead," Angela said quietly.

"Our psychic antennae for each other are always up. Know what I mean? We *seem* to be drawn to each other for obvious reasons--looks, personalities, all kinds of mutual attractions. But in many cases, I think with us, there's something more.

"I feel that you're trying to *lock* us in place without really knowing who *I* am--"

"You're swimming in water that's too deep for me, Micki. Can't we walk along the shore? I only asked you up for a cup of coffee."

Micki checked her watch, sat silently for a few seconds, then said, "Don't you remember that I have something of yours?"

64

"My mother's watch, yes."

"It's very beautiful," Micki replied, "and now I feel I know why you treasure it so. Thank you for being so honest with me. I know it's not easy to talk about losses."

She reached into her bag for the envelope in which she'd placed the watch, ran her thumb and finger across the folded paper, and held on to it rather than pass it to Angela.

"If you like, I'll drop it off at our jewelry department tomorrow morning. They'll replace the safety chain."

"That's very nice of you, Micki."

"I've tried as best I can to explain--" Micki began.

"Don't you *want* to come up? Just for a cup of coffee. It doesn't have to be anything else."

It was difficult for Micki to give an answer.

Angela chattered on. "I haven't got much in the way of food, but I can make omelets and a salad. And I've got a bottle of white wine chilling in the frig."

Micki took the key out of the ignition. "Coffee," she said firmly.

Angela smiled. "You're going to like my place, Micki. I haven't been here very long, so you're one of my first guests. I'm still decorating, but it's definitely livable."

Micki locked the car, followed Angela across the street to the stylish four story brick townhouse. When Micki fell a step behind, Angela grabbed her hand, as if she was afraid Micki was going to change her mind.

Inside the apartment, Micki looked around. "Nice," she said, nodding in approval of stark white walls and a look that could best be described as minimal.

A large glass coffee table was the major focal point of the living room. Turquoise and navy blue directors chairs were arranged around it. In a corner, across from a window that looked out on an ailanthus tree, was a long Haitian cotton sofa. Scattered across the sofa were magazines and books, shoes, a bathrobe. Angela walked over, grabbed them in her arms, opened a door, threw them in.

"Why waste time on house cleaning?" she asked.

"Why, indeed?" Micki answered.

From where she was standing in the living room, Micki could see a small efficient kitchen and beyond that doors leading to three other rooms.

"Big place," Micki said. "You live here all alone?"

"I do...and even if I wanted a roommate, I'm not sure it'd be so easy for me to find one with the kind of schedule I keep. So what'll it be?" Angela asked. "Wine or coffee?"

"Now that I'm up here, let's have a glass of wine," she said, settling into a corner of the sofa.

"I don't know much about wines, Micki, but the bottle that's chilling is supposed to have a wonderful bouquet."

"If it's wet and cold, we'll give it five stars. And how about an ash tray?"

"Tough order to fill...I ain't got any!"

"Do I have to step out into the hall for a smoke?"

"No, I'll bring you a saucer," Angela said cheerfully, as she stepped into the kitchen.

When she returned with the bottle and glasses on a tray, her hands were shaking. She was nervous.

"Everything all right?" Micki asked.

"I had a bit of a problem with the corkscrew. I got it to work, though...and here's a make-shift ash tray. Just give me a sec to open a window, it's stuffy in here."

Angela opened windows on both sides of the apartment, then from the small mosaic tray she took the bottle and looked at the label.

"I hope it's all right."

Micki swirled the wine in the round goblet, held it to the light. "Looks wonderful, Angela. So, whom shall we toast?"

"Let me think," Angela replied. "How about us?"

"Us?"

"Us."

"To us."

They raised their glasses and drank.

"How *is* the bouquet, Micki?"

"Superb," she smiled, setting down the glass. "You did well for such a novice," she said smiling.

"I wanted something you'd like."

"How'd you know I'd be tasting it?"

"I didn't....I bought it Friday on my lunch hour. I was hoping you'd come up after the ride back. Is there anything wrong with planning ahead?"

"Angela, I wasn't trying to criticize you before--"

"Don't worry, you're here, that's all that matters. Now what do you think? Like the apartment?"

"Yes, very much."

Above a corner filled with ferns and tall dracenas were photographs of Angela interviewing various public figures. On another wall, arranged in a horizontal line, were six framed documents, awards that Angela had won.

"You've done well for yourself," Micki said, nodding in approval.

"Thanks," Angela replied.

Micki sat back as she listened to Angela talk about her hopes for being hired by one of the network stations in New York. Excitedly, she elaborated on her plans for the future and Micki gradually relaxed. She began to feel secure in the knowledge that with Angela, her career came first. Micki had no doubts that she would achieve all of her goals.

Time had passed quickly. Angela poured the last of the wine into their glasses.

"It just so happens, there's another bottle chilling in the--"

"No more," Micki said softly. She reached for Angela's hand, shook her head no. "I want to make love," she said quietly, directly.

Angela looked at her and said nothing. Micki moved closer held Angela's face in her hands, kissed her on the lips. Angela responded, then pulled away.

"You're not interested?" Micki asked softly.

"Oh, yes...but now, I'm nervous."

Micki laughed. "You're the one who extended the invitation, remember?"

"Of course, it's just that I'm afraid of making mistakes, of doing the wrong thing. I want you to care--"

"Ssssh," Micki urged, "stop worrying."

With her fingertips, Angela began to massage Micki's forehead, her temples, cheekbones, the line of her jaw. At the same time, she kissed each spot she touched. Micki reached for Angela's waist, but Angela shook her head no.

"Let me give you pleasure, let me please *you*," she said as she unbuttoned Micki's blouse. She buried her face in Micki's flesh and sighed softly.

Micki looked down at Angela; there was an expression of peace on her face, of satisfaction and tranquility. She was seeking sustenance as much as making love.

Wherever her mouth roamed, she left tiny love-marks. Then Angela kissed her on the mouth, her tongue slowly tasting the inside of Micki's lips.

"Come to bed with me," Angela implored.

Micki didn't want to move, didn't want to interrupt the passion that was growing. "Stay here with me, don't leave," she pleaded.

She brought Angela's mouth to hers, kissed her urgently. She didn't want to let her go, but Angela pulled away, stood beside her.

When Micki reached out to touch her, she stepped back, pulling her shirt high over her head, her breasts arching toward upstretched arms. She brought her hands down over her face and body, caressing her own breasts before stepping out of her shorts.

Naked, she looked down at Micki. Then she straddled Micki's body as she offered her breasts. It was only for a second though, a tease.

She eased Micki out of her shirt, slid down the length of her body and unzipped her slacks. She nuzzled Micki's stomach, pulled Micki's slacks off, threw them on the floor beside her.

She knelt beside Micki, her hands and mouth exciting, teasing, loving Micki, who gave herself up to Angela's desires.

Micki felt a gentle warm glow within. She sighed, exulting in the exquisite pleasures of the moment. She moved ever so slowly with Angela, following her wherever she led. She lost herself in Angela's love-making and wondered why she had ever hesitated where Angela was concerned. The question didn't need an answer now. She closed her eyes, ran her finger tips across Angela's shoulders, twined locks of hair about her fingers.

Suddenly, unexpectedly for Micki at that moment, the intensity of the soft, mellow glow increased, exploded, and jewels of passion, hard, hot, pulsating, coursed through her body. She cried out, held Angela close, cried out again.

They lay quietly for awhile as Micki gently caressed her. She smiled at Angela's eyes, clouded with desire. She kissed her, wiped a trace of dampness from Angela's face. "You're a passionate lover, Angela, do you know that?"

"I am?"

Micki sat up, propped herself against the cushions. "Most definitely," she said. Micki's expression was curious as she looked at Angela, thinking about what she'd earlier told her about herself. "Isn't there some place more comfortable for us now?"

"Oh, yes," Angela said, taking Micki's hand and leading her from the sofa.

An oversized waterbed dominated her bedroom. Large plants in plastic tubs had been placed near windows, and pictures of Angela hung on all four walls. Micki took a closer look. Angela wasn't doing any interviewing in these.

"These the ones your friend took?"

"Some of them. There's more, if you're interested in seeing them."

Most of the photos were nude studies. Micki took her time looking at the various poses.

"What would you do if the wrong person got hold of these?" she asked.

"I have the negatives and these are the only prints Karen made."

"How do you know?"

"I wouldn't take a chance on something like that."

"I can see why," Micki said, sitting on the bed, bouncing lightly on the buoyant mattress. "Do you float to paradise on this or ride the high seas?"

"Whichever you prefer. How about some more wine?" Angela asked.

"Now? No, I think we've had enough."

Angela seemed nervous again. Micki reached for her, gently took her hand.

"Come here, Angela, lie down beside me. Let me hold you."

Angela's expression was shy and strangely uncertain, but as Micki lay back, she sat down next to her.

"Angela," Micki said softly, "talk to me. Tell me about your lovers. Who was your favorite? What was she like? What was her name?"

"What makes you think I've had so many lovers?"

"Haven't you?"

She shrugged. "I make the people I'm with very happy. I know how to satisfy, don't I?"

"That you do...but who have you loved?"

Angela shook her head. "No one. Who says going to bed with someone is the same thing as loving?"

"It's an old-fashioned idea, don't mind me."

"What's the big deal?" Angela asked, irritated by Micki's questions. "You mean to say *you* don't fuck unless you're in love? I don't believe it!"

Micki's expression registered surprise at Angela's tone, her language. "That's *not* what I mean--"

"Look, Micki, you probably don't want to make love to me at all. I *do* know how to satisfy, I *never* get any complaints. But when it's my turn, nothing happens. Zero. I *fake* it and I'm a damn good actress--"

"I don't believe you. What about our dance at the Blue Moon? You weren't feeling anything then?"

"A freak accident, even you'd agree to that. What else can I say? I don't want you to be disappointed in me."

Micki looked at Angela. Sitting there next to her, she could have been a statue. The expression in her eyes was cold, distant, her body was tight. Micki sensed control in every muscle.

Angela turned to Micki and smiled. Like ice. Micki was determined that she would make the ice melt.

"You've just had me, Angela," Micki said deliberately, "now I'm going to have you. And don't think I'll be satisfied with the deep freeze."

Micki reached for Angela's arms and pulled her down beside her. She lay on top of her, wrapping her legs around Angela's, pinning her arms to her sides. Angela began to shake her head back and forth, tried to break free, but Micki wouldn't let her go. She pressed her body against Angela's, a violent sense of urgency driving her toward possession. Then, slowly, she felt Angela's body relax beneath hers and she freed her arms, loosened her hold on Angela's legs. She lifted her body and leaned a few inches above Angela, their nipples barely touching.

"Maybe no one else has been this to you before," Micki said, "but I'm going to be your lover." She hesitated for a second, surprised by her words.

Then she kissed Angela gently this time, their passion growing until Micki could feel Angela's hands running up and down her back, scratching, pulling, holding her tight.

"Take it easy, Angela," she whispered. "We're going to take our time tonight."

She began to kiss Angela, traveling the length of her body, beginning at the top of her head and moving to the soles of her feet. Her hands teased whatever they touched, lavishing love, coaxing arousal. When she felt Angela's passion rise to meet hers, she pulled back, she paused. Then, just as Angela seemed to rest, she began again.

Angela reached for Micki's hand, tried to guide it toward her. Micki resisted, wanting Angela to wait even longer.

Now she caressed her gently. Lightly, she licked Angela's face, the tip of her tongue tracing patterns from her chin to her forehead. Her tongue searched out the hollows in Angela's ears as Angela wound her legs around Micki. Their bodies were salty, covered with light, glistening perspiration.

Micki absorbed the aromas of sex and sweat and nuzzled under Angela's arm, licking the gently rounded globes of her breasts. Micki watched Angela's nipples harden, grow darker, and in a pattern of light, teasing bites, she circled the flesh of her breasts.

Then her face rested on Angela's stomach, her hands grazed Angela's thighs, fingers weaving in and out of dark, curly hair.

As Micki began to touch her, she sensed a damp darkness she might have encountered in the deepest of cool rain forests.

Angela began to murmur soft sounds, sweet pleadings, as Micki lowered her face upon her and drank the dew of her flesh. Her tongue played lovingly, bringing Angela close to climax, then easing her down again. She made love with her hands until Angela cried out with pleasure. Still Micki didn't stop and Angela's cries grew louder as Micki lowered her mouth upon her once again. Angela arched her back to bring her body even closer to Micki's. She began to move in a rhythm that Micki followed.

As if from very far away, Micki began to hear Angela's low, sobbing cries. Then as her body reached the heights that Micki wanted her to know, Angela's voice pierced the night. Her back rose in a graceful arch that Micki supported with the palm of one hand. Angela fell back and Micki touched the tears of release now streaming down her face.

Micki tasted the tears, cradled Angela in her arms and rocked her gently back and forth. The younger woman clung to Micki, then tore herself loose, turning on her stomach, burying her face in her arms.

Micki touched her back, followed the line of her backbone with her fingers, brought her hand up to Angela's shoulders and gently kneaded muscles that suddenly were tight, tense.

"You're upset," Micki said gently.

"I'm not," Angela said, turning to cover Micki's face with kisses.

"Then what is it?"

"I don't know. Maybe it's just that it was never like this for me before. Never. You felt it too, didn't you?"

"Yes."

"You were just so *good* to me, Micki. We made love, oh, how we made love. I'll remember tonight forever."

Micki held her close; it seemed that now it was time for sleep.

"Don't you want more?" Angela asked, suddenly alert.

"More?"

"I don't want to sleep, Micki. I want to keep the night alive."

"Isn't it almost time for morning?" Micki asked, feeling a sudden exhaustion.

Angela pointed to a clock. "It's not even midnight! And what about dinner? I'm *starved!*"

"Omelets now?"

"Why not? I can whip them up in seconds."

"Sure," Micki said in friendly resignation. "Make your omelets."

Micki was counting on a few minutes rest, while Angela prepared the meal. She closed her eyes for what seemed no more than seconds, then Angela returned.

"We've got something better than omelets," Angela said, pouncing on the bed.

Micki looked up, saw that Angela held a hand mirror, a hollow gold cylinder, a razor blade, a small white packet.

"I think I'd rather have eggs," Micki said tiredly.

"Oh, no, Mama. You did something real special for me tonight, so I going to return the sweet kindness."

"Angela, I'm not interested in *any* kind of drug, count me out--"

"It's snow, Mama, pure, sweet snow. With this, we'll be making *love*--notice I said love---when the sun comes up!"

"You're going to be making love to yourself, sweetheart. I'm not having any. And stop calling me Mama!"

"Sure thing, Mama," Angela said teasingly, leaning over to kiss Micki's breasts. "So come *on*, I can't believe you've never tried coke before."

"And I'm not starting now. You don't know what's in that stuff. Anything you buy on the street's been cut so often you might as well shell out a hundred bucks for a gram of baby powder."

"A hundred and forty. But this stuff ain't baby powder, it's *beautiful*. I've had some. Watch me, then just try a little. If you're

73

real good, I'll put some in a special place and send you right off to your favorite planet."

"No you won't, hands off where I'm concerned."

"It's not so much fun alone," Angela said, opening the packet and sprinkling a generous amount on the mirror. She set the mirror down between her legs, carefully refolded the packet and slipped it under the bed. Performing a familiar ritual, she began to cut the coke until it was fine white powder arranged in four even lines on the mirror.

"Watch me," she said, inserting the gold tube in her right nostril. She inhaled, breathed deeply, held her head back and closed her eyes.

"Micki, trust me. This is something you are going to like."

Micki watched the expression on Angela's face. She lowered her head and it seemed as if every muscle in her body relaxed.

"We're here together, come on. The worst thing that can happen is that you won't feel anything at all. That's the way it usually is the first time.

"Look, watch me. Just remember to breathe as deeply as you can. Take it all the way in, in a few seconds you'll begin to taste it at the back of your mouth. Swallow then and inhale some more. All you can."

Angela sighed with delight. "Come *on*, give it a try."

Micki shook her head no as she looked at Angela. Where had she seen such black eyes before? They were chips of mica, nuggets of ebony, black stars set in a white sky.

Micki was disappointed, hurt that the passion they had just shared wasn't enough. Why did Angela crave this high? Why at this moment? And why with drugs?

She thought about getting dressed, leaving. She tried getting up from the bed, but once more found herself entwined by Angela's needs.

"I want you again," Angela cried. "I want you to lose yourself...I want you to be *me*."

Micki reached out to touch Angela's face and Angela took her fingers in her mouth, biting and sucking, as Micki watched, transfixed by her intensity.

They came together and continued, one leading, the other following, then both of them in unison, on and on, passion carrying them to heights neither woman had known before.

And when it ended, there were no tears from Angela this time. Only silence. Only peace. And Micki forgot everything else that had happened except their lovemaking.

They lay quietly, each touching the other's body gently, fingers running over the insteps of feet, over ankle bones, around toes. It seemed to both of them that there was something new and wonderful about it all...

Night, now grown pale and shallow, was leaving the summer sky. A new day was beginning.

CHAPTER 7

Micki was awakened by Angela's light touch, fingers tracing patterns across her back. She opened her eyes and lay still for a moment or two as she slowly took in what she could see of the room around her. Then she turned to look at Angela.

"Morning," Angela said cheerily. "You don't mind if I eat breakfast in bed, do you?" She waved a leafy stalk of celery in Micki's face.

"No," Micki said, kissing her good morning, "just don't offer any to me."

Micki snuggled close to Angela. No two mornings will be alike, she reflected. She smiled, thinking of the variety and novelty of mornings to come. Feeling reasonably awake, she reached for her cigarettes.

"Not first thing in the *morning*," Angela complained, burying her head under the covers.

"Aren't the windows still open? Let some good, clean city air absorb the smoke."

Micki pulled back the sheet, placed a tender kiss on Angela's forehead. "I hate to mention this," she said regretfully, "but I have a feeling I'm running late. What time is it?"

"Barely seven, there's no need to rush. We have all day, don't we?"

"Oh, how I wish," Micki replied. "By the time I get back to my place, shower, change, it will be close to nine. I have a nine-thirty appointment with my staff."

Angela didn't want Micki to leave. She told her to call in sick or to take the day off.

Micki laughed at her pleas. "What time are you due at the station today?"

"Not till four...I've got the late shift this week."

"Good for you, but there's no such thing for me. I'm going to have to hustle as it is."

"When will we see each other?"

"I'll call later this morning and we'll make plans."

Micki did want to stay with Angela, but she kept moving, gathered her things, got dressed quickly.

She paused as she stood at the door, then said, "It was wonderful, Angela. Every minute of it. But I've got a feeling I'm going to be paying for it today. When you climb back into bed, take a nap for me."

Angela watched Micki drive away. When the car was out of sight, she sat down on the bed. She fingered the sheets, held a pillow in her arms, wanting any essence she could capture from the night.

I knew she'd come back here with me, Angela thought, I knew it. We're just so right for each other, she has to want me the way I want her. It was so *good* last night...for both of us.

A tremor coursed through her body, a shudder of pleasure brought a smile to her lips. I knew I could please her, she reflected, but Micki, she was...the best...she let me experience everything...everything I've ever wanted to feel with a woman, everything I've dreamed about.

Angela paced the room exultantly, jubilant, excited, high. "We can be *everything* to each other, I know we can," she said aloud.

She smoothed the sheets then shook the spread, the fabric billowing over her head. She was positively giddy as she made the bed. She belongs to me, she told herself, I know it. She'll never want to leave me now, why would she?

The heady confidence, the absolute lightheartedness of her feelings stayed with her as she showered and dressed. She turned on the TV while she scanned the morning papers. The news of the day held no interest for her as she waited for the phone to ring. By ten, she'd grown impatient. She dialed Hewitt's Department Store. The line was busy. With the next call, she was told that Micki was out on the floor. When she dialed the third time, the message was that Micki was at a sales meeting.

She asked to speak with Ms. D'Allessandro's secretary, explaining that she was Micki's niece and a family emergency had occurred. It was important that she be reached.

Angela was assured that her message would be delivered immediately. She hung up and waited for Micki's call.

"What's wrong?" Micki asked in a concerned voice a few moments later.

"I'm lonely," Angela said pleadingly as she blew kisses into the phone.

Micki's voice was tense as she began to speak. "Angela, this has been one of those days when I haven't had a minute to myself. Meg said you phoned four times this morning. Why so often? I told you I'd call; you don't have to play games. And what's this about being my niece?"

Angela laughed lightly. "Don't be so *serious*, love, I just wanted to invite you to lunch. My treat, Auntie. And don't be mad."

"I'm not *mad*, Angela, I'm busy," she said firmly.

"Don't you miss me?" When Micki didn't answer immediately, Angela said, "See, you *do* miss me, admit it."

Micki didn't want to encourage Angela, but the truth of it was that, in spite of her busy schedule, her thoughts had been on little else that morning.

"I have to get back to the meeting, Angela," she said, ignoring the question. "I'll call you as soon as I'm free, I promise."

"Are you near a window, Micki? Take a look at the day we've got for ourselves. Looks like the sun is shining down from heaven just for us. You want to see me, I know you do. Let's meet at Quincy

Market, by Faneuil Hall. That's only a short walk for you. You pick the restaurant, but let's eat outdoors."

When Micki didn't respond to this, Angela continued, "You *do* take a lunch hour, don't you?"

"Yes," Micki said, won over by Angela's persuasive tactics. "Meet me at one o'clock, we'll eat at Lily's."

Enjoying her crab meat salad and iced tea, Micki did her best to strike a serious tone with Angela, but Angela refused to pay any attention.

"I keep my professional and my personal lives separate," Micki said, "I always have."

"May I quote you on that?"

"Angela, would you like it if I called you a half dozen times during an interview? Wouldn't you find it unnerving?"

"I'd *love* it, Auntie. Call any time you like."

Micki shook her head in mock exasperation. "I give up. And *stop* calling me Auntie!"

"You're the first Micki I've ever known," Angela replied thoughtfully. "I like the name, but somehow, it doesn't seem to suit you. What's it short for...or is it a nickname?"

Micki smiled. "My maiden name was Foley. I was christened Margaret Ann but my friends started calling me Micki when I was just a kid. The nickname stuck, and when I married Guy D'Allessandro, it seemed to fit...better than Margaret."

"That explains it," Angela said. "Now it does make sense. But Auntie's cute...Aunt Margaret."

"Cut it out," Micki threatened jokingly.

Angela agreed that she would and then smiled at the waiter who approached their table. He was no exception to the majority of people who seemed to recognize Angela that afternoon. Micki was impressed by her manner, her graciousness. This was a completely different Angela from the childish prankster who had playfully arranged their meeting for lunch.

They lingered over coffee, enjoying this time together. The afternoon was passing pleasantly for them both.

"It'll be after midnight by the time I get home, Micki. Will you wait up for me?"

Micki was surprised by Angela's question. The thought that they'd be seeing each other that evening hadn't yet occurred to her.

"Tonight I'm going to bed real early, Angela. And by myself. Take a good look at my eyes. Notice the puffiness? Some of it's from the wine we drank, but mainly it's because I had only a few hours of sleep."

"Most people wouldn't complain," Angela teased.

"Right, they wouldn't," Micki said, "but you've got to listen to what I'm saying. You're zipping along in a pretty fast lane right now, and maybe you think you're young enough to get away with it. A few years from now that won't be the case. The camera will pick up every trace of weariness, every trace of wear. If you think this question is out of line, don't answer it, but how often do you take drugs?"

Angela leaned across the table, her voice an intense whisper. "I *don't* take drugs. What are you *talking* about?"

"Last night, don't you remember?"

Angela brushed bread crumbs from the table, her gesture impatient, angry. "Someone I don't even *know* left that in my apartment. I thought you'd find it a turn-on. Plenty of women would."

"Then you don't--"

"Of course not," Angela interrupted. "That's something you'll never have to worry about with me."

Micki leaned back in her chair, gauged the truth of Angela's comments from the expression of her face. "I believe you, but don't forget, Angela, moderation. Learn it now."

"You weren't so interested in moderation last night," Angela said, looking across the table with sexual directness that made Micki lower her eyes, even blush.

But when she looked up, Micki responded to Angela's comment with an expression in her eyes that said she agreed.

"How about it?" Angela continued. "You'll have plenty of time to catch some sleep before I get there. I'll buzz twice so you'll know it's me. I'll bring a midnight snack...pastrami sandwiches and potato salad."

"No snack for me."

"Then you do want to see me tonight," Angela concluded with a positive smile.

"Ring twice," Micki replied.

******

Micki had napped and bathed and now lay on her bed in front of the TV watching the eleven o'clock news. Angela's segment had been filmed at the New England Aquarium late that afternoon. She stood at the end of a dock, sky, sea and billowing sails behind her, completing a feature story on summer visitors to the popular spot.

As the camera caught Angela in a close-up, Micki determined that she would exercise control with her, that she would not let things get out of hand. She believed her about the drugs. She was convinced that the cocaine Angela had in her apartment had no doubt been left by someone who had visited her. Micki questioned why a woman as ambitious as Angela would possibly jeopardize her future by even experimenting with drugs.

She had no answer, but she concluded that it wasn't a subject for concern. What did worry her, even as she looked forward to Angela's arrival that evening, was the insistent drive Angela possessed to obtain or manipulate anything she wanted. As much as Micki desired her, her feelings at this stage were tentative and questioning.

Aware, though, that Angela would soon arrive, Micki stood and looked at herself in the mirror. She ran the comb through her hair, glossed her lips and loosely tied the sash of her red silk robe. A few minutes later, she heard a light tapping at the door.

She walked over to the viewing device in the center of the door. Seeing no one, she called, "Who's there?"

"The big, bad wolf," Angela replied stepping up to the glass circle.

Micki undid the chain, opened the door. "How'd you get up here?"

"One of your neighbors just *happened* to recognize me. Wanted to know if I had time to stop off for a drink. I told him I had a previous engagement. Hey, I brought you roast beef instead of pastrami. I know there are people who just can't *stand* pastrami. Where's the kitchen? I'll drop these on some plates."

Micki gestured toward the rear of the condo while Angela looked about the room.

She let out a low whistle. "Look at this, would you? What do you do? *Own* the store?"

"Let's just say I paid my dues in a marriage that lasted too long."

"Then let's *enjoy* all this bounty," Angela said, rushing to Micki's open arms.

The next four weeks passed quickly. The only nights they spent apart were those when Micki was in New York buying for the winter season. She came back with leg warmers and mittens for Angela, hardly a gift she expected with temperatures hovering near ninety. Micki told her to put them away for a cold night in December; it would come soon enough.

One afternoon, Angela invited Micki to the studio to watch the taping of a feature story. Her professionalism was evident in all that Micki observed. The research, writing, setting up, and the many takes, all were taken in stride.

This was yet a different Angela from the impulsive woman Micki had come to know. When they were together at home, she acted like a kid. There was charm to this side of her personality, but Micki found herself preferring the Angela she now observed at work.

Maybe they did have problems, but they didn't seem to be insurmountable, Micki convinced herself. True, Angela still plagued Micki with phone messages, especially when she was in New York, but she no longer pulled stunts on Micki's office phone.

Angela's moods still troubled Micki, though--the irrepressible highs, the sullen lows. She tried to understand the cause. Was it drugs, pills, some chemical substance...or was Angela's personality even more complex than she presumed?

Cut it out, she told herself. Stop analyzing everything. She's young...she's still got a lot of growing up to do.

At the present moment, Angela's major interest focused on the idea of giving up her own apartment and moving in with Micki. Micki had given her several reasons as to why this would be impossible.

"I've grown used to my privacy," Micki had insisted. Angela only laughed at this.

"Relationships take time to develop," Micki commented. Angela shrugged and looked at her watch.

"There's the difference in our ages," Micki had said, finally. "Twenty years, after all."

At this, Angela held Micki close, gently caressed her and whispered, "I'm yours."

Micki's real doubts, though, were not put into words. Angela was headed for a career that would take her far beyond the human interest stories she was doing so well for a local TV channel. And though Angela was fascinated with Micki now, absorbed by her, Micki did not believe their relationship would last. One day, someone else was bound to turn Angela's pretty head and Micki knew that there was nothing she'd be able to do to stop it.

Why, then, invite the pain that would be part of this? Why speak of this to Angela? Why not simply enjoy what they had?

They left the studio together and when she and Angela arrived back at the apartment, Micki hurried to answer a ringing telephone. Noelle was calling with the news that Lana and Ruth were getting married the following Sunday.

"Sounds as if it'll be *the* social event of the summer," Micki said. "Where's it taking place?"

"North Truro, on the beach, with the reception at the Blue Moon. Lana said to tell you she's sorry she didn't send wedding invitations, but the local women's press folded and she didn't want to take her business elsewhere."

"Loyal to the end," Micki chuckled. "Who's giving the bride away or have they dispensed with such mundane conventions?"

"I don't know all the details yet, but Lana and Ruth are very serious about it all."

"And they should be, Noelle," Micki responded. "I only asked because lesbian weddings are new to me. I've never been to one before."

Micki glanced at Angela as she sat down, picked up a news magazine. "And, oh, Noelle, I'll probably be bringing Angela with me."

"Is that so?" Noelle replied. "Fine. Well, drop in when you arrive and I'll give you directions to the house in Truro."

Angela raised her eyebrows. In a perturbed voice, she inquired, "What happened? Did she drop the phone when you told her I'd *probably* be coming?"

"Not at all, we'd finished our conversation."

"I'll bet," she replied angrily.

"*Now* what is the matter?"

"There's still *something* between you and Noelle, I can tell, and I don't like it."

"Yes, we *were* lovers...over a decade ago...but I've told you all of that. She's my *friend*, Angela! What do you mean you don't like it?"

"I don't...and don't think you're putting anything over on me."

Angela's jealousy had surfaced before over a woman who had called one evening while Micki was in the shower. Micki had been patient with Angela that evening, but tonight she wasn't in the mood. She didn't feel like placating her unwarranted and irrational response.

"I'd like you to come with me," Micki said evenly, "but if it's going to be a problem for you, I'll go down alone."

"I'm sorry," Angela said, "I just don't want you with anyone else."

"Angela, when do I have time to even *see* anyone else? If I'm not *with* you, I'm talking to you on the damn *telephone*! I hope Noelle will always be my friend, I've told you that. But now that we're on the subject, where are *your* friends...your old lovers?"

"I never claimed to have a stable of ex-lovers," Angela exploded. "That's your specialty! I have friends...the people I work with...Gary...there are others. Maybe I've been too busy with work to take the time to cultivate the kinds of friends you're talking about."

"You're *that* busy," Micki asked cynically.

"You're damn right I am," Angela insisted. "Any time I decide to, I can make all the friends I want. That still doesn't mean I'm going to trust Noelle."

At this, Micki began to laugh. "I can't take you seriously," she said. "Come on, Angela, let's go to bed."

When Micki walked out of her apartment building Friday afternoon, she was surprised to see Angela leaning against her car. She'd planned to pick her up in the South End.

"What are you doing here?" she asked, giving Angela a quick kiss on the lips. "Didn't I tell you I'd swing by?"

"I cut out early, walked on over."

"Why didn't you ring the bell and come up?" Micki unlocked the car doors, stashed their gear in the trunk.

"Didn't you ever think I might get tired of ringing the bell? What am I? The Avon lady?"

"Hop in," Micki said. "I'm sorry it's an inconvenience. What do you want to do? Fly up?"

"Give me a key; spare me the trouble of growing wings."

Micki pulled out into traffic without answering Angela.

"Are you afraid I'll have the place ripped off?"

Micki concentrated on her driving.

"Micki, we're lovers. We sleep together every night. You have a key to my place--"

"Which I never use--"

"But you have it, don't you? And do you mean to tell me none of your other lovers had *keys*?"

"Believe it or not, they didn't. Angela, you just about live with me now. Let's leave things as they are. No key."

"You don't treat me right, Micki," Angela complained.

Micki shrugged her shoulders, lit a cigarette. Angela rolled her window down and turned her attention to the heavy traffic.

As they approached the expressway, Angela said, "I couldn't stop thinking about you today." She rubbed the back of Micki's neck, continued speaking, her tone passionate, insistent. "All I wanted was to be with you...for us to be together....Do you know what I mean?

Don't you want that, too? Making love is all I think of anymore. It keeps getting better and better for us, doesn't it?"

"You know it does, Angela."

"Then let me have the key," Angela pleaded.

"No, no, no, *no*," Micki insisted. "Angela, I know it's not the way you want it to be, but I just don't think we've known each other long enough. Besides, I'm so used to living alone, so used to my own privacy, my own time, that it's hard for me to think of functioning differently."

Angela's expression suddenly changed, as she realized Micki was not about to give in...yet. "Whatever my sweet Mama needs, whatever my Micki wants," she answered saucily.

Once situated in their room, Micki began to hang up her clothes, arrange her toiletries. Angela did her usual thing: threw clothes over a chair, scattered cosmetics over the top of the bureau and left her opened suitcase in the middle of the floor. Then she stretched out on the bed like a cat.

"Comfy?" Micki asked, sitting down beside her.

"Hmmmmmm," Angela purred.

Micki looked around the room. "Just like home," she chuckled. "Angela, how *do* you manage to look so neat? Your clothes are rolled up in *balls* on the floor!"

"Body heat," Angela replied in a sultry voice. "It presses them."

Micki smiled, lay down beside her, ran her hands through Angela's thick hair. "I can't seem to get enough of you," Micki sighed. "One of these days it's got to peak."

"No," Angela insisted with emotion. "We're going to go on forever; I've told you that. We'll get better and better. We'll *never* peak."

Micki wrapped her arms around Angela, held her passionately. They kissed and slowly, tenderly, Micki caressed Angela's face. She kissed her eyelids, her brow, her cheeks, the tip of her chin. She nibbled on sweet, tiny ear lobes.

"Still interested in dinner?" Micki whispered teasingly.

"Uh huh...but later...not now."

"We'll do it all later...have dinner, get directions for tomorrow's wedding...sound all right to you?"

"*Much* later," Angela insisted.

She reached out and pulled Micki's shirt up over her head, unzipped her jeans, pushed the clothes on the floor, slipped out of her own garments as quickly as she could.

"In a hurry, darling?" Micki asked.

"What makes you say that?" Angela replied as Micki's mouth and hands roamed her body. "Make me a necklace of your kisses," she whispered. "Circle me with love."

Micki buried her head between Angela's breasts, breathing in an essence of perfume that exuded heady passion.

"My beautiful orchid," Micki said, "my flower."

Playfully, she nipped Angela's flesh, "I'll pick a bouquet of you, press you...like a flower."

"You're hurting," Angela squealed. "Don't bite so hard."

She grasped Micki's buttocks, wrapped her legs around Micki's calves, succeeded in flipping her over.

"Now let's see how *you* like it," she said, pressing her breasts to Micki's, pushing her hand between Micki's thighs. Her caresses were urgent, fierce at first, then when she felt Micki respond to her touch, they became soft and melting. "Raise your knees," Angela murmured, giving Micki room to move, "open wider."

Angela's fingers penetrated quickly, furiously, deeper and deeper, as Micki's warm flesh urged her on. Her hand moved to a rhythm they both were feeling. Micki reached out, pulled Angela close, groaned in ecstasy as waves of pleasure swept over her body.

"So *who* picked the flower?" Angela asked teasingly.

Micki smiled. "Anyone knows you need more than one posy for a bouquet," she responded, holding Angela in her arms.

The next morning, Angela dressed for the wedding. She wore a strapless white sundress, loosely tied a silk scarf covered with daisies about her neck.

Micki reached for the scarf, pulling Angela close. "You look lovely," she said admiringly.

"You approve?"

"You've taken my breath away, you're exquisite--"

"But not neat, remember?"

"I'll take you as you are."

"You will?"

"Yes." Micki opened the slider, looked out at the crimson dawn. "What a magnificent beginning to the day, and not a cloud in the sky."

She stepped to the dresser, brushed her hair, tied a striped sash around the waist of her deep purple shirt.

"We're going to enjoy the day, Angela," she said brightly, "every minute of it."

"You've got the wedding fever...wonderful! When are we going to tie the knot?"

"Us? Angela, don't you know the problem with knots? They're just too hard to *untie*. Let's be happy with what we have."

"I am, but I want more," Angela said, then kissed Micki on the mouth.

Cars spilled over from the pebbled driveway to both sides of the dirt road leading to the large cedar shingled beach house. Micki pulled in at the end of the line.

"A *major* event," Angela said excitedly.

"Then you are going to have fun today?"

"Did you ever doubt it, Mama?"

"*That* you're going to have to cut out, I'm not fooling."

"Why? I don't think of you as being sensitive about your age."

"No? Maybe not, but I am old enough to *be* your mother and perhaps today I just don't want to be reminded of it."

"That's silly--"

"Let's join the others. I don't want to miss the beginning of the ceremony."

They walked toward the guests who had gathered in a semi-circle on the beach. Noelle and Jessie stood off to the side, Jessie softly strumming her guitar. They wore long billowing white blouses over white slacks. Micki waved to them and Noelle smiled back.

There was a sudden hush in the murmur of the crowd as people turned to watch a tall woman in white walk toward a linen draped lectern.

Noelle began to hum a melody over the chords from the guitar. Then Lana and Ruth stepped from the house, walking together, smiling at their friends. Noelle began to sing, softly at first, then her clear, strong voice filled the morning air with a song of love.

Lana took Ruth's hand as they stood before the minister. They turned to face each other as she began the ceremony. Lana was striking in a white tux, ruffled shirt, bow tie. A thin satin ribbon ran down her pants leg to gleaming patent shoes. Ruth wore a flowing pale lilac gown, a lace veil covered her hair. She looked shy, tender. As the vows were spoken, they exchanged rings, kissed, then turned to face the crowd. Lana beamed proudly at Ruth and acknowledged the hearty applause by raising their clasped hands in the air.

"Glad we're here?" Micki asked. Her eyes glistened with tears as she applauded.

"It was lovely, yes."

They followed the crowd indoors for a traditional champagne toast. Micki looked about the room, pleased to see several familiar faces.

"I didn't realize I'd see so many old friends today," she said cheerfully.

"And I don't know a soul," Angela sullenly replied.

Micki watched the expression on Angela's face. Very quickly, as often happened with her, her mood changed. She was pouty, a bit angry.

"Then I'll just have to introduce you to everyone, love," Micki said lightly, not wanting any part of the day to be spoiled.

A dark-haired woman in a cocoa linen pants suit walked over, hugged Micki, held Micki's hands in her own.

"Evy," Micki said "how *nice* to see you."

"It's *been* a while, hasn't it, Micki?"

"A few years, yes?"

"You can't remember any better than that? How passion fades."

Micki pulled her hands back, reached for a cigarette, was momentarily uncomfortable.

"You look wonderful, though. Something...or someone...must be agreeing with you."

"You're right about the *someone*," Micki said. "Let me introduce you to my lover, Angela Hall."

When Evy didn't respond, Micki continued. "What's the matter? Don't tell me this is the first autumn-spring relationship you've seen, Evy," she said defensively.

"That's not it, Micki, don't be foolish. It just took me a minute to place you, Angela. Channel 8, right? I like what you're doing. The piece last week on the new theater company was fascinating."

"Thank you," Angela said quietly.

Angela wanted to move on, to get Micki away from the conversation that was now going on. After all, it was clear that at one time, she and Evy had been more than friends.

Fortunately, Lana and Ruth, about to make a toast, now became the center of attention in the room.

A waitress from the Blue Moon bearing a tray of champagne walked over to Angela.

"Champagne?" she asked.

"Yes, thank you," Angela said, her gaze lingering as she smiled into deep blue eyes.

"Don't forget to come back," Angela said flirtatiously. "One glass is never enough."

Noelle now joined Lana and Ruth as they stood in front of a large stone fireplace. Glasses were raised as she toasted the happy couple and all joined in.

Evy turned then and raised her glass to Micki, wished her good luck, walked on into the crowd.

Micki took Angela's arm, speaking in a cool, stern voice. "Don't flirt with other women when you're with me, Angela. I don't like it."

"Oh? But I'm supposed to grin and bear it while your old lovers line up to pay homage to you?"

"Stop it. Evy and I knew each other a long time ago. Our paths rarely cross now, I can't even remember the last time I saw her. You didn't have to be quite so cool with her, did you?"

"You don't seem to like *anything* I'm doing today," Angela said angrily. "How long do we have to stay here? This group bores me."

"You're being very unpleasant, do you know that?"

"We don't *belong* here! These women all look so...old," Angela said.

"You really think a comment like *that* is going to get you anywhere? If anything, most of them are younger than I am."

"But you don't *act*...middle-aged--"

Micki smiled in spite of being annoyed by what was happening. "Angela, I *am* middle-aged, so you better get used to it. And stop *pouting*! You're jealous and possessive when there's no need for it! Don't spoil this day."

"That woman just...I just didn't like her."

Micki laughed. "Who says you have to like everyone I've ever known?"

"If we leave soon for the Blue Moon, we'll beat the crowd," Angela said sweetly as she took Micki's hand.

Closed to customers for the day, the Blue Moon had been transformed into a circus tent of crepe paper streamers and gold and silver balloons. A lavender banner had been draped above the bar proclaiming: Lana and Ruth--Happiness Forever.

Jennifer, the club's disc jockey, had chosen medleys of traditional wedding songs that greeted the guests as they arrived. The bar tables had been covered with snowy tablecloths, and in the center of the room was a large table which held the four-tiered wedding cake.

They walked toward the bar and Angela asked for Scotch.

"I've never seen you drink Scotch before," Micki said quietly.

"Nothing's worse than a champagne hangover. I don't want to risk that."

Jessie and Noelle soon arrived and as Jessie and Angela quickly became involved in a discussion about a possible TV spot, Micki joined a group of women from New York whom she hadn't seen in a while. Connie and Pat, Barbara and Carol, couples who had been together for many years, were standing with Evy White and a woman named Donna.

"See what we missed by being born twenty years too soon?" asked Evy.

"Yep," replied Connie, "it's a brand new world for these babes and they don't even know it."

"But our experiences are priceless, aren't they, girls?" asked Barbara, and they all laughed, remembering what life had been like for lesbians when they were young, talking about what they jokingly described as the good old days.

Angela joined them a short while later, champagne glass in hand.

"Thought you didn't want a champagne hangover," Micki said, surprised to see that Angela was already on her second drink.

"I forgot how *strong* Scotch is. After three drinks, I started seeing double."

"Three? They must have been *fast* drinks. Why don't you switch to coffee?"

"Oh, let's go," Angela said impatiently, "we've paid our respects."

"So soon? This party's probably going to go on all day, all night. They're starting to put out some food. Why don't you get something to eat? And look, Lana and Ruth are having a ball at the reception line. It's starting to thin out. Why don't we go on over?"

"You go, Micki." Angela's voice was cool as she said, "Give them both a big hug and a kiss for me."

"Angela," Micki said, her patience coming to an end, "if this is *so* unpleasant for you, go back to the room! Here's the key--"

"I don't want to, I'm just not in the mood for a wedding. Unless it's ours. Anything wrong with that?"

"We'll straighten this out later," Micki said. "I don't want us having this kind of argument in front of all these people. We're *guests* here, have you forgotten? And do me a favor, Angela, stop the drinking...right now."

Angry, Micki walked quickly across the room to the reception line. By the time she made her way to Lana and Ruth, however, her mood had changed.

"Congratulations," she said warmly as she hugged them both, "I hope I'm around for your 25th."

"We're *so* glad you're here?" Ruth replied. "Where's your little friend?"

"With Angela, there's always someone who wants to talk to her."

"Of course," Ruth said sweetly. "She's a *celebrity*. Would she pose with us for one of the wedding pictures?"

"I'm sure. And Ruth, you look lovely, you both do."

Lana grinned, reached for Ruth's hand, kissed it tenderly. "She does look great, doesn't she, Micki?"

Micki agreed, kissed them both, wished them good luck and walked off to find Angela. When she finally saw her, Angela was with the young blonde waitress who had served the champagne after the ceremony. They were both laughing and as Angela took yet one more glass of wine, Micki's temperature began to rise.

"What's happening?" she asked, taking Angela's arm.

"Oh, hi, Mama. Heather was just telling me a very funny story. Heather, tell it to Micki."

Heather shook her head and looked down at the floor. Then she raised her eyes, flashed a smile at Angela and said, "I have to keep circulating, but I'll see you later, okay?"

"We'll be here till the party ends," Angela called after her.

Micki said nothing. Then Angela broke the silence.

"You want me to socialize, don't you? After all, this *is* a party and parties are for *fun*, aren't they? You've been having fun, Micki, catching up on all the news with your old girlfriends, making dinner dates to reminisce about *old* times. You're having your share of fun, why shouldn't I?"

"Okay, let's get going. You've made your point."

"We can't go now," Angela said petulantly. "I haven't even kissed the brides. Loosen up. Laugh. Have some champagne."

"Slow down! Am I going to have to carry you out of here?"

"No, but Lana's going to carry Ruth over the threshold, that's for sure. Hey, there's another one of your old *friends* waving to you. Better go see what she wants. Maybe she's planning a class reunion."

"Your humor's wearing *pretty* thin, Angela."

"I love you, Micki, you know that?" Angela wrapped her arms around Micki's neck, gave her a long, drunken kiss. "I guess I had one glass too many of the bubbly stuff. You're not mad at me, are you?"

"Angela, *stop*...or you won't be standing when they cut the cake."

"I'll have coffee now, I promise. Black." She kissed Micki again and walked in the direction of the large silver coffee urn.

Soon, Micki was joined by her friend, Beverly Keating. Micki registered surprise. "Hey, I didn't know you were a regular at the Blue Moon."

"I'm not," Bev replied, "but Lana and I go way back."

They chatted in an easy fashion, but Micki's attentions were on Angela. She watched her take a cup of coffee, begin to drink it, then look over, wave to Micki, set the cup down, and walk out to the deck where Lana and Ruth had gone.

Concerned when Angela didn't return, Micki tried to end the conversation with Beverly several times, but Bev continued her stories. Finally, Micki was able to break away. She walked out to the deck, where Lana and Ruth were celebrating with several of the guests.

Lana's expression was happier than Micki had ever seen it. Then quickly it changed. She took Micki's hand, pulled her close. "Don't stay with that one," she said softly. "Find someone else."

"*What* are you talking about?" Micki said, wrenching her hand from Lana's clasp.

"She's on a journey, Micki, and she wants someone with her every step of the way. *You* don't have to go along. Drop her."

"What journey?"

Then Lana gestured toward the short flight of stairs that led down to the beach. "It's not just what's going on *now*," Lana said pointedly, "it's everything about her."

Slowly, Micki walked across the deck and to the steps.

Angela and Heather, the waitress, were sitting on the stairs, Angela a step or two below Heather. Her arms rested comfortably on Heather's knees.

How do I break up *this* little party, Micki asked herself, without throwing them both into the sea?

Then Angela's hand touched Heather's shirt and she flirtatiously played with the top three buttons.

Micki stepped forward, called Angela, who turned, stood, began to follow Micki. Micki headed straight for the exit of the Blue Moon.

As they got into the car and began the drive back to the Inn, Micki gave in to her anger. "You want to fool around, do you, Angela? Keep this up and I'll show you what fooling around's *really* like. Don't you *ever* think you can carry on like that again--"

Micki turned to look at Angela. Her eyes were closed, her head rested against the side window. She'd either passed out or fallen asleep.

It wasn't long before Micki pulled into the parking lot at the Inn. "Angela," she called loudly, "Angela, you have to wake up. Come on, you can do it."

Angela groaned, shook her head no.

"I can't carry you, Angela. Let's go, out of the car, on your feet."

"Not going anywhere," Angela muttered. "Want to sleep right here. With you. Let's sleep right here."

"Come on, Angela, I'm taking you to the room."

Micki walked around to the passenger's side and opened the door, turning Angela's legs, pointing her feet to the ground.

"You can do it, Angela, one step at a time. We'll be there in no time. Stand up, put your arm around my neck. Think you can make it?"

Angela groaned and held on tight as they walked toward the Inn. Micki decided to avoid the main entrance. Slowly, they made their way around the back of the motel to their first floor cabana room. Micki unlocked the slider, led Angela to the bed, laid her down. She took off her high heeled sandals, brushed hair back from her face.

"How're you feeling?" Micki asked in a loud voice. There was no answer. Standing up, Micki walked to the door, slid the screen across and stood looking out at the tranquil blue water.

"Angela," she called. Still there was no answer.

Micki walked to the bed and sat down. She reached over and pulled the spread up, not wanting Angela to be chilled by the cool breeze that was blowing into the room.

"You're going to have some hangover," she said softly.

The anger had passed. For the moment. She'd save the lecture for tomorrow. Now, she leaned back on her elbow, lit a cigarette, and watched Angela sleep.

"You're out for the night, aren't you baby?" she said a few minutes later. "Some big-time make-out artist you are. It's a good thing I rescued you from that friend of yours. Not that there was ever any chance of my letting you go off with her. That's one thing you're going to have to learn, Angela. When you're with me, it's full time. That's it. Period. No part time work allowed. And why would you want any? Don't we have a good enough time together, just the two of us? Aren't I enough for you?" she asked quietly.

Angela reached for a pillow, curled herself around it.

"What a beauty you are," Micki said, pulling the sheet up over Angela's bare shoulders. "But you know that, don't you? You're bright, talented...young. What can I give you anyway? Where would we go together, the two of us? You're going to hit the big time, baby. Soon. Then all of a sudden, whatever this is all about for you won't mean that much.

"But I love you. Do you know that? I love you, Angela. I've fallen in love with you. Believe me, I really didn't plan for that to happen."

Micki gazed tenderly, watching her lover sleep. A few minutes later, she asked, "Still in dreamland?"

She got up from the bed, reached for a note pad and a pen, wrote a short note for Angela:

Hi, Sleepyhead,
    In case you wake up before I return, I've gone back to the
reception. Take two aspirin and stay in bed. See you soon, love.

She placed the note on the night table where Angela was sure to see it when she awakened. For a moment, she wondered whether she should stay, but it was still mid-afternoon of a beautiful day and Angela would probably sleep for several hours. Why not return to the wedding party?

She walked into the Blue Moon to the sound of clapping hands. A circle of women stood on the outer edges of the floor while in the center Ruth and Lana danced to a polka, whirling each other about, kicking their heels, laughing, singing along in a frenzy of happiness.

Then the music changed and a chorus of women began to hum the "Anniversary Waltz" as Lana led Ruth in yet one more dance. Suddenly a hot disco beat drowned the waltz and the dance floor was crowded with exuberant women dancing along with Lana and Ruth.

*****

Angela slept deeply, then later dozed and dreamed and grew restless when she no longer heard the reassuring sound of Micki's voice.

"Micki," she called, her eyes still closed. "Micki, come be with me."

When there was no answer, she tried to sit up. A bolt of pain shot through her head.

"Oh, my God," she groaned, and then carefully lay her head back on the pillow. She stared at the ceiling as the room began to spin, ever so slowly. She reached out to hold the mattress, then clutched her stomach, closed her eyes and lay still.

"Micki," she called out weakly, "I think I'm going to be sick."

She sat up, squinted in the direction of the bathroom, aimed herself that way and reached the toilet just in time. She couldn't stop the contractions in her stomach. One chilling spasm followed another until there was nothing left to regurgitate and she lay on the floor and cried.

In time, she sat up, propped her back against the tub, reached for the toilet paper and blew her nose. She wiped tears from her cheeks, but with her eyes now wide open, the room was no longer spinning. She stood, steadied herself by the sink, then slowly walked back to the bed and stretched out face down.

As if from a dream, they were all there. The blonde waitress. Micki. The car. The struggle to get back to the room, her arms wrapped around Micki. Micki talking, sitting near her, covering her, patting her shoulder.

"Micki, where *are* you?"

Angela looked about the room. "Micki, I remember what you were talking about. 'I love you,' you said, 'I'm in love with you.'"

Then she saw the note. "Aspirin? Stay in bed? After what you've just told me? No way, Micki."

Streams of pulsing hot water poured over her body as Angela stood under the shower. Steam filled the shower stall. She breathed deeply, was cleansed, felt purified. She shut off the hot water, forced herself to stand under the cold, then dried herself briskly, a new woman.

Her hair still wet, Angela folded a bandanna into a narrow ribbon and tied it around her head. She slipped into a pair of fresh white shorts, a red cotton T-shirt, and stepped into her running shoes.

"I'll jog that mile and a half to the Blue Moon," she said.

*****

Micki and Beverly were standing out on the deck watching the last streaks of red light from a brilliant sunset in the early evening sky.

"It's time I got back to the motel, Bev."

When Micki turned to the doorway, she saw a familiar figure framed in darkness, a silhouette, walking toward her.

"What are you *doing* here?" she asked in surprise. Then she caught herself. She didn't want Angela to think that she had so quickly forgotten all that had occurred that day.

"I didn't think you'd be awake before noon tomorrow," she said sharply.

"Tell me," Angela said softly.

"What?" Micki asked in a quiet, firm voice.

"Tell me what you told me back in the room. I know I wasn't hearing things."

Angela was out of breath, perspiring, but smiling. "Come on," she pleaded. "I want to hear those words again."

Angela stepped close and as Micki felt herself being captured by the expression in her eyes, she knew that in spite of all her protesting, her conditions and defenses, she could no longer deny the truth of her words.

"I love you," Micki said simply, shaking her head back and forth in wonderment.

"And?"

"And.." She paused, placed her hands tenderly on Angela's shoulders. "And...I'm in love with you."

"I love *you*, Micki...so very, very much," Angela echoed softly. "You forgive me, don't you?"

Micki smiled, "Yes."

"Everything that happened was only because I was jealous of all those women you were--"

"Angela, the world's not going to stop turning for us. They're my friends. They're not going to disappear because I'm with you. And neither is anyone else going to disappear."

Micki directed Angela's attention to Heather who stood a few feet away, an expectant smile on her face. Angela looked at her as if she'd never seen her before and Heather turned and walked toward a group of women.

"That was cruel of you," Micki said.

"No, it wasn't. Anything else would have been, though."

"I see. I'm still surprised you're here, I was just on my way back to you when you walked into the room."

"You'll give me a lift, won't you? I don't know if I have the strength to jog both ways."

Micki smiled, "Sure, the party's going to break up soon anyway."

"You think so? It looks as if Lana's just getting warmed up. What do you say we have a dance before we go? They're playing lots of slow numbers now...that is, if you don't mind dancing with a jock."

"Some jock," Micki said.

Out on the dance floor, they closed their eyes, danced slowly to the music, an incongruous couple: one so young, the other middle-aged, one dressed for play, the other for a party, one fair, one dark. Now, they moved as one.

All too soon, they were interrupted. "May I cut in?" Lana called out in a booming voice.

After the long day, she looked a bit wilted. She'd taken off her bow tie, unbuttoned her ruffled shirt. Her cummerbund drooped dismally around her waist, but her smile was broad and her spirits were high.

"Of course," Micki answered, offering her Angela's hand.

"I thought I'd dance with you, Micki," Lana said, reaching to take her in her arms.

"I need to catch my breath. Angela's the one who's raring to go, aren't you, love?"

Angela cast a dark look, Lana looked flustered, but Micki brought their hands together.

"I want you two to get to know each other. Who knows? You might end up as bridge partners some rainy night when there's nothing else to do."

"I never play cards," Angela said coolly.

"Me either," Lana said. Then her face lit up with a smile. "So what the hell, Angela, let's dance. There's a great polka coming up."

Micki walked back to a seat at the bar and turned to watch them. Lana threw herself into the dance, swinging Angela back and forth across the floor. Soon Lana crossed her arms in front of her chest, squatted, did her best to hop and kick at the same time. Angela looked impatient, as if she was about to walk away, but suddenly Lana reached for her, as much for support as anything else, and the two of them fell to the floor, Lana rolling on top of Angela.

Then Lana and Angela were both laughing, along with the rest of the women on the dance floor. Quickly, Angela regained her balance and helped Lana to her feet. Someone slid a chair across the floor, which Lana immediately sat in, pulling Angela down on her knee. Lana spotted Ruth, called her over, sat her on her other knee. Ruth gave Lana a kiss and in an impulsive gesture, Angela did the same. Then she hopped off Lana's lap and returned to Micki.

"I didn't *know* you were such a dancer," Micki said in good spirits. "What style, what grace--"

"Let's go before anything else happens. She still wants to dance with you."

"Lana seems perfectly content with Ruth right now."

"I was so embarrassed when we fell," Angela exclaimed.

Micki laughed. "View it as your punishment, my sweet?"

"For what?"

"Have you forgotten your little friend so soon?"

"As a matter of fact, I have."

"Good," Micki said as they walked toward the door arm in arm.

CHAPTER 8

Candles on the dining room table cast a lovely glow on gleaming cherry wood, which reflected shimmering images from the warm flickering light. From her comfortable chair, Micki enjoyed the view both inside and out. She gazed out the window toward the dark blue ribboned Charles River separating Boston from Cambridge. A stream of steady traffic flowed on either side and headlights shone in the dusky twilight. To the west, the setting sun, a bright red ball of fire, slipped behind the buildings silhouetted on the horizon.

Micki had looked forward to a leisurely dinner at home that evening. She had spent much of the afternoon preparing the meal which, on Angela's plate at least, was getting cold, going uneaten.

"Something wrong with dinner?" she asked with concern. "It's all right," Angela replied disinterestedly.

"Have some salad; the tomatoes taste every bit as good as home grown."

"I still have some."

Trying to coax Angela out of her mood, Micki continued, "This should be your kind of night, Angela...just the two of us, candle light, a romantic setting, no other commitments for the evening, my best attempt at a gourmet meal...what's wrong? Did something happen at work?"

"It was an okay day," Angela said flatly, "nothing out of the ordinary."

"Let me humor you a bit more, my darling. We're having fresh strawberries for dessert."

"Keep my portion in the frig, Micki. I promised some friends from work that I'd go dancing with them tonight."

Micki leaned back in the chair. "Are you trying to annoy me?" she said sharply. "If you were going out, why didn't you let me know earlier? I could have had dinner with someone from the office or fixed something easy for myself."

"It was something I decided on at the last minute. When I got here, I could see you'd gone out of your way to plan something special. I didn't want to spoil it."

"And you think you haven't?"

"I'm eating your dinner, all *right*? The fish is over-cooked, I'm allergic to tomatoes and the rice is gummy...Is that what you want to hear?"

"No, Angela, I want to hear about what's going on with you," Micki said indignantly, as she began to clear the table. Her hand was shaking as she picked up the dishes and she realized how upset she was by Angela's behavior.

Angela shrugged her shoulders, passed Micki her uneaten salad. "I'm starting to feel like a recluse since I hooked up with you," she said pointedly.

"You haven't complained about the lack of companionship before," Micki said as she sat back down. "Why is it a problem so all of a sudden?"

"I need a night out with some friends, Micki," Angela replied coolly, distancing herself from the conversation.

Micki was hurt by Angela's response, yet at the same time she was curious as to what was going on. Had they isolated themselves from others so completely, or was she simply giving in to a sudden whim?

"Will I see you later," Micki asked quietly, "or will you be going back to your place?"

"The West Newton Street apartment I have? Yes, I'll be there tonight...and every night from now on, Micki."

Micki reached across the table, grabbed Angela's hand. Her tone was insistent, demanding, "What *is* this all about? You've *got* to tell me what's going on."

"Take a guess...oh, never mind," Angela said flatly, "I'll tell you, but I don't expect you'll do anything."

"What is it?" She gripped her hand all the tighter.

"It's pretty simple, Micki. I'm starting to feel used," Angela responded as she glared across the table.

"Used? How? What are you talking about?" Micki's tone was incredulous.

Angela pulled her hand back. "This is a one-sided relationship, Micki, even you must see that. I'm tired of it."

Micki smiled, but only slightly. "You feel *used*, is that it?" The tone of her voice rising, she continued, "Have you ever thought that I might feel the same? This is your second home now, isn't it? Yet what do you *do* here? When's the last time you offered to pick something up for dinner? Or to *do* something around here?"

"I *don't* view our relationship as one-sided, Angela, but I think I know what this is about. You still think you can strong-arm me about moving in here, don't you? Just forget it...go out dancing...every night, if you want. Stay over on West Newton Street if you think you'll be happier there, but don't try to manipulate me!"

Angela stood and began to pace the room, hurling her words at Micki. "I don't like what you're saying, Micki. There is no reason that you have yet explained to me as to why we're not living together. There aren't even any excuses...not the age bit, you've used every bit of mileage on that one, our jobs, any future job change I may make. What *is* it? Lovers *plan* for the future. I want to share my life with my lover...with you...can't you *understand* that?"

"We do share our lives--"

"It's conditional! I don't like it. I'm warning you, I'm not going on like this. It isn't fair and I don't need it. Find yourself another playmate from the far side of town."

"You're not a playmate--"

"The *hell* I'm not," she shouted. "You want to know something else, Micki? I've come to the conclusion that it's your problem, not mine...'cause I'm moving on.

"I'm starting to understand a few things about you. You are one frightened, superficial woman, you know that? Sure, you've had lovers before me...probably more than you've ever told me about...and they've put up with you for a while...maybe not as long as I have, but no doubt they were more experienced with women like you. They all moved on, didn't they? Well, so am I...unless I get a commitment from you--"

"On *your* terms---"

"Of course! Are my *terms* so outrageous? They sound very *normal* to me!"

Once again, Micki tried to explain her point of view. They had all the time in the world to make commitments, to live their life together. Why the rush?

"Angela, we have so much. Don't give it up over something as silly as--"

"A key? It's not the *key*, Micki. It's that I want us to *be* together. By not giving me the key, you're doing to me what I think you've done to everyone else--keeping me locked out. Nobody gets the key to *you*, Micki, am I right?"

Micki paused before speaking, then delivered her words slowly, deliberately. "You are not going to push me into something I'm not ready for...something I don't want--"

"Why don't you want it? In plain English, you're just too scared to share."

Micki waved her away. "Go out and dance, Angela. You'll feel differently in the morning."

"So will you, Micki, believe me."

During the argument, Micki had tried to keep her feelings under control. With Angela gone, thoughts raced through her mind.

"What the *hell* does she want a *key* for? She already lives here," she said, striding out to the kitchen, a stack of dishes in her hand. "Pop psychology is for TV specials. She's not going to force me into this!"

Micki slid the dishes across the kitchen counter, walked to her bedroom, picked up a new mystery novel and angrily cracked open the cover.

She slept soundly that night, awoke refreshed. It was pleasant to take her time with the morning paper, a relief not to have Angela reach for the pages before she'd finished.

Micki enjoyed the quiet, prepared a leisurely breakfast. She didn't like conversation in the morning, she realized, whereas Angela started chattering as soon as her feet touched the floor.

Micki moved to the wide, cushioned living room window sill, sat and watched the morning traffic crawl along the Charles River drives. She felt a heady euphoria at having her house back again and only once before she left for work did she consider calling Angela.

By week's end, however, she was surprised that Angela hadn't called or, as the days had passed, hadn't shown up, leaning on the bell, as she so often had in the past, until Micki pressed the buzzer which opened the foyer door.

She realized how quickly she'd come to enjoy the somewhat unorthodox routine she and Angela had established. She felt *comfortable* having a lover, a partner, being coupled with Angela. Then, too, Micki enjoyed being her mentor, took pleasure in this kind of interaction with Angela.

She turned on the late news and sat miserably in front of the TV watching the cool beauty who had been her lover. She stared at the image, looking for signs that Angela was distracted or unhappy, but she was at her best. Micki hit the remote control angrily and Angela's presence vanished.

An hour later, still awake and wanting desperately to call her, she grabbed the phone, then flung it back in the receiver in disgust.

At one-thirty, she was still awake. She looked at the over-flowing ashtray, reached for another cigarette. The pack was empty.

She knew she wasn't about to sleep at that point. She reached for a pair of jeans and a sweater, drove to a nearby all-night store, bought her smokes, lit up and then, without thinking about what she was doing, drove into the South End.

As she drove down West Newton Street, she looked up at Angela's apartment. The lights were on, but she kept moving.

It was after she'd driven around the block three times, waging as strong a fight as she could with herself, that she accepted that she was going to give in to Angela.

She realized there had been no other thought in her mind that week--she *wanted* to give in to Angela. All of the reasons she'd been so clear about earlier were meaningless without Angela. She admitted that her hesitation, her stubborn resistance centered around her own fears.

And how fair is *that*, she asked herself. How can I expect Angela to understand my fears of losing her? Would *anyone* accept that as a reason for setting up these barriers?

Maybe it *is* only a matter of time before she leaves for New York...maybe she *will* find someone else...move on, but what am I gaining by *not* living with her? And what does *that* guarantee? Nothing.

I know she *needs* me. She's put up a strong front, but she's fragile. I can guide her, take care of her. No one has the answers to the future so why don't we just try to work with what we have now?

The various factors Micki had defined as obstacles in their relationship began to crumble. We'll deal with the difference in our ages on a day by day basis, that's the only realistic way. After all, I'm far from being a relic, she told herself confidently. And Angela will *mellow*, she convinced herself. She's got a *good* head on her shoulders; she's not going to risk her career because of drugs...or any other kind of madness. Finally, Micki admitted that she had never known this kind of love before, this kind of passion. It was all a part of Angela...and she didn't want to lose a single piece of it.

With her mind firmly made up, she looked for a parking place. The only free spot was several blocks away. She eased the car in against the curb, checked her pocket for the small change she'd picked up before leaving her apartment, and walked quickly, the now familiar commentary running through her mind every step of the way. Cold night air stung her face. She lowered her head, hurried on, finally turning the corner to Angela's block and the building she now lived in.

She rang the bell. There was no answer. She stood with her hands jammed deep in her jeans pockets, fingering coins, small objects. She rang again.

She was about to leave when she heard the voice on the intercom.

"It's me," Micki said in response, "buzz me in."

"Open the door yourself, you have a key." Angela's voice was a hollow echo, exaggerated by the quiet of the night and the raspy reception from the intercom.

"I forgot it, open the door," Micki said urgently.

"It's late--"

The buzzer cut off Angela's words, Micki pushed the door open, quickly climbed the stairs to the apartment.

Once inside, Micki looked at Angela tentatively. There was no expression of victory, triumph or even happiness on her face.

"Couldn't sleep?" Angela asked flatly.

Micki reached into her levis, pulled out the key. As she spoke, her voice trembled in anticipation of Angela's response. "This is what you want, isn't it, Angela?"

Angela waited for Micki to approach her. "Is it what you want?"

"Yes," she said firmly, "it *is* what I want. Take the key, Angela."

"We're together, the way we belong," Angela whispered, reaching for Micki and the key at the same time. "I've waited for you to come...I want you *forever*."

A cold shiver passed through Micki as Angela held her in a fierce embrace.

"Yes, you do, Angela, you do," she said, holding Angela just as tightly, not ever wanting her to escape. Not ever.

CHAPTER 9

Angela let it be known at the station that she was giving up her apartment, that she was looking for the right person to sublet it until the lease expired. Within a week one of the news writers had seen it and was making arrangements to move in at the end of the month. Angela was jubilant.

Micki and Angela had already discussed various potential problems, but agreed that it was best to handle them as they occurred, rather than try to anticipate difficulties.

During the first weeks they lived together, they settled into an easy, comfortable relationship. Angela was sensitive to anything that Micki seemed to need and Micki responded similarly. Then, gradually, there was chaos again, the kind that previously Micki had been happy to leave behind at Angela's apartment when she returned to her own home base. That space was gone now.

Micki tried to be patient about the noise and clutter. She solved part of the problem by asking the woman who cleaned for her to come once a week, rather than twice a month. There didn't seem to be any way, however, to solve the differences in their energy levels. Micki needed her eight hours of sleep a night, there was no way to change that. And she also needed quiet times by herself. This had become almost a necessity after living alone for the years that she had.

Micki had no regrets, though, about having Angela as her live-in lover. The good times they had together made it worth it, even though the buying trips to Manhattan that used to be big city

109

adventures for Micki had now become a welcome chance to catch up on some lost sleep. Micki had often been told that she had energy to burn, but compared to Angela she was a dying ember.

As the months passed, the rough edges of adjustment to what was a new situation for both wore off. There were minor differences, including Angela's fad diets, but nothing they weren't able to sort out and solve.

With Angela, however, when she was taken by a new idea, she accepted it wholeheartedly and with fervor. Without telling Micki, she decided they should both become vegetarians and gave away all the meat in the refrigerator and freezer.

"Why keep temptation under our noses?" Angela had asked. "We'll feel healthier when our systems are free from the influence of having eaten flesh."

"*Flesh?*"

"What else is meat but animal flesh? Do you want to go on eating fried flesh?"

Next she told Micki that it was time to eliminate all alcoholic beverages from their diets.

"I want us to be *pure*," she had said. "Don't forget, I accepted your guidelines concerning no drugs."

"Angela, nothing could have made me happier," she said approvingly. She laughed heartily. "The next thing you'll suggest we give up is sex--"

"No way! In fact, making love is *why* I want us to keep our bodies pure. Our bodies should be sacred temples, the envelopes of our souls--"

"See you later, sweetheart. This temple's been around too long to care about being sacred."

And soon enough the fads passed. They were nothing more than a part of Angela's eclectic personality. Interests taken up one week were dropped, usually a short time later.

Trying to see the good in this, Micki had told herself that though the quality was exasperating at times, it probably was one of her lover's strengths as a reporter.

Angela took her assignments seriously, did the research, immersed herself in the story, then quickly moved on to what was given to her next.

To those who knew Angela casually, she was a whirlwind of energy and excitement, bright and enthusiastic, one of a kind, really.

Micki, however, observed how difficult it was for Angela to slow her pace. She seemed frantic in her desire to know or to please, almost as if there was no escape for her, nor any lasting satisfaction. And Angela so rarely experienced what Micki told herself was normal fatigue, that Micki began to suspect she was using uppers. When asked about it, Angela assured Micki that she was drug free, in every way. Any experimentation she'd indulged in the past was over.

To the outsider, the fads, the fleeting interests were charming, but Micki was gradually reaching the conclusion that anxieties propelled the younger woman's frantic searching.

For the moment, Angela's base of security was Micki. How long, Micki wondered, could she give Angela all she needed?

As Micki checked into her hotel room late on a Monday afternoon, she was handed two messages. The first was from Angela; she knew enough to expect it. She was surprised by the second, which was from Noelle. She sat down, propped her feet up on a coffee table, dialed her number.

"How did you know where to find me?" Micki asked, happy to be talking to her old friend once more.

"Easy, I tried to reach you at work today and your secretary told me you were in New York and gave me this number," Noelle replied.

"Everything all right?"

"Perfect, things are going real fine for us. I'm flying to Boston for an audition this Friday; thought I'd drop in and say hello. But since you're here, Micki, how about dinner at my place tonight?"

"Give me an hour or so to unwind and I'll be over. An audition in Boston? Where?"

"I'll tell you about it this evening. There'll be just the two of us for dinner. Jessie's in Rhode Island visiting her family."

"We'll catch up on what's happening then."

She'd no sooner hung up, when the phone rang. It was Angela.

"Who were you talking to?" she asked abruptly.

"Noelle called and we're having supper together tonight. I haven't seen her since this summer--"

"Her? Where's *Mrs*. Music?"

"Don't be sarcastic, Angela."

"Who's cooking? Jessie or Noelle?"

"Noelle. Jessie's visiting folks in Rhode Island."

"How cozy. You better not make any funny moves, Micki--"

"You're being ridiculous."

"Don't go to Noelle's."

"Angela, she called to say she has an audition in Boston this weekend. We'll all get together then if you like."

There was silence on the line. Then in a soft voice, Angela said, "What's her number? I'll call you there later."

"I'll be back here early enough. Call me then."

"Fine," she said sharply. "And have a *nice* reunion...it'd probably bore me anyway."

"I think you're right...and what are you up to tonight?"

"I'm working on a feature story...about a woman living in northern Vermont. She's ninety-six and still painting...supposed to be another Grandma Moses. I might drive up to interview her next week. Want to come along?"

"I'll try, Angela."

"Love me?"

"Of course," Micki said.

"Not as much as I love you," Angela responded.

"Angela, I'm in *love* with you. There's no way to measure love---"

"Am I supposed to take your word on that?" Angela laughed. "Okay, have fun and give my best to Noelle. I miss you."

"I will. And same here."

As they sat on the comfortable over-stuffed sofa, Noelle took Micki's hand.

"You look exhausted, Micki. Are you working too hard these days?" she asked with concern.

"Actually, now that I think of it, the past month's been rather slow. What is it? The circles under my eyes? I'm not wearing makeup, Noelle, you're just seeing...me."

"I know *you*, Micki, it's not the lack of makeup. You're too thin...frankly, I've never seen you looking this tired."

"If I do, thank my lover. It must be the same with you and Jessie. She *is* a few years older than Angela, but I'll bet she runs you around in circles."

"Not at all, Jessie's very laid back. We have a quiet life, really. A movie, dinner out maybe once a week, now and then an art show, music, of course. Probably sounds dull compared to the pace you and Angela keep."

"It's the pace *she* keeps, Noelle, not me. Maybe it's our diets. Three months ago, we were vegetarians, then we switched to fruit and fiber, now it's the Cambridge diet." She laughed. "Come on, *everyone* wants to be thin. I thought you'd compliment me on my slim figure.

"I think you've overdone it. Besides, why do you follow her fads?"

"Noelle, when Angela takes up something new, it's just easier to go along with her, believe me."

Noelle passed Micki a plate of cheese and crackers.

"She's that persuasive?"

"Yes."

"Dinner tonight will be quite ordinary then--"

"Whatever it is, it smells delicious."

"Roast chicken, oven braised vegetables, a simple meal."

"Marvelous."

"And homemade apple pie for dessert."

"You haven't always been this domestic, have you?"

"Oh, yes. In P-town, I put so many hours in at the club that I didn't have time to do the everyday things I enjoy. There's nothing very exciting about it, though...whereas you, you're living with a star.

She's going to make it *very big*...but I worry about her where you're concerned. I have since you two first met."

"Why?" Micki asked, "what are you talking about?"

Noelle leaned back in her chair, thought for a moment before speaking. "She'll be a star, for sure," she said, "but like a comet, she'll burn herself out in the night sky."

"Angela? Funny you should say that. There are times when we're together, I feel more like the comet. Just before it makes its plunge into eternity." If Micki's expression revealed weariness, her tone conveyed bewilderment.

"Is that the way you want to feel?" Noelle inquired.

"*Want* to feel? Who knows? I've never been involved with someone like her before. My style's always been to partake and enjoy, but not to immerse myself."

"You can't be in love unless you do," Noelle said.

"Then I am in love, because with Angela, I'm nothing if I'm not immersed."

"But that in itself shouldn't cause problems," Noelle continued, aware that she was probing. "I don't think you're telling me everything."

"What else do you want to know? I've tried to explain the differences between us, but it's something beyond that, Noelle. In the beginning, I was quick to blame Angela's recreational use of drugs--"

"Recreational? What if it's more serious than that?"

"It never was! Besides, she's totally drug-free now."

"How do you know?"

"I have eyes, don't I? Aside from being at work, we're with each other all of the time...and I trust her. That was one of the conditions of her moving in with me...no drugs. She agreed without hesitation." Micki's tone became defensive as she continued, "I don't believe drugs ever *were* a problem with her...just one more form of experimentation for Angela. Something new to try."

"Are you sure you're not protecting her by denying what might still be going on?"

"Why do you continue with this?" Micki asked indignantly. "I told you she's not on drugs; it's not that. It's something else I can't quite put into words."

"Try," Noelle said encouragingly.

Micki looked around the room, taking in various paintings, pieces of pottery, a photograph of Jessie and Noelle.

"She walks a thin line, " Micki said softly. "That's all I can tell you right now."

"And can you handle it?" Noelle asked gently.

Micki reached out for her friend's hand. "Yes, I can, Noelle. There's no reason for you to be so concerned."

"But if problems do develop, will you get help?"

"I promise you I will," Micki replied earnestly. "I want this to work with Angela."

"*You* can't solve her problems, Micki, remember that, "Noelle said emphatically.

"All right, Noelle." Micki changed the subject, not wanting to continue the discussion about her relationship with Angela. "Now what about you? Are you happy?"

Noelle's answer was in her smile.

"Then we're both lucky, aren't we?" Micki asked.

Angela's phone calls didn't begin until after dinner. By the third call, Micki's patience had reached its limit.

"Angela," she said angrily, "what *is* wrong?"

"When will you be back at the hotel? I don't want you staying there. I don't trust Noelle. She's looking for the chance to start something up again with you, I know--"

"I'm here for dinner, I'm not *staying*, " Micki said slowly, trying, as she had in the previous calls, to allay Angela's anxieties, though she was rightfully annoyed.

"Why isn't Jessie there? What's the real reason? Have they broken up?"

"What you're doing now isn't fair--"

"Why not? I'm your lover."

"Yes, you are my lover, Angela--"

"But now you're with her--"

"I'm going to ask Noelle to unplug the phone--"

"Don't--"

"I'll call you when I'm back at the hotel."

"Don't unplug the phone. I won't call again, I promise. But you will call me as soon as you get back?"

"Of course."

"You won't forget? Micki, I...I don't know what to do when you're not here."

Micki remembered the many other trips she'd made to New York when she and Angela had touched base by phone several times without these kinds of problems arising. Angela had never been upset in quite this way.

"I'll call as soon as I get in."

Micki replaced the phone and shook her head. "I'm sorry, Noelle," she said apologetically.

"Is she always this frantic?" Noelle asked, pouring a cup of coffee for Micki.

"Not always," she replied.

"No wonder you're so tense. To be honest, I couldn't take that kind of pressure."

"She's insecure. She's worried that I'm here with you alone... that Jessie's somewhere else."

Noelle smiled understandingly. "Well, whatever the reason, it would drive me to distraction."

"Believe me, Noelle, even after her performance for you this evening, I do and can control her...at least where her outbursts are concerned. She *won't* call back."

"*Good*," Noelle said. "More coffee?"

"No, thanks, I've got an eight o'clock meeting tomorrow morning, so I should probably head back to the hotel."

"I'd like you to hear our tape, do you have time for that?"

"Of course."

Noelle played the tape she and Jessie had made, then a tape of her own songs which she'd recorded in French. Micki leaned back and listened to melodies that were haunting and sad.

"Love songs," Micki said, "they must be."

"Some of them are."

"They're lovely. Why don't you release these songs?"

"It's the old story of finding the right market. I thought I had one company interested, but in the end, they said they couldn't take a chance on an unknown performer. They suggested I come back when...how did they put it?...I make a name for myself."

"You will, Noelle. And appearing in Boston is sure to be a step in that direction."

"Maybe, but there are more important things in life than success--"

"Such as?"

"Peace of mind, for one."

"Ah, yes, but you don't pay the bills with peace of mind."

"I've always been able to pay my bills...in spite of not being a great success."

The tape ended and Noelle smiled at Micki. "You need to get going, don't you?"

Micki stood, reached for her bag and answered, "Yes, I do."

Back in her room, Micki dialed Angela's number.

"That was a hell of a long supper," Angela said. "What did you do? Have the hostess for dessert?"

"What's all the noise?" Micki asked, ignoring her question.

"A little music...a little conversation. I figured why sit here by myself tonight, so I called a few people, mixed up a pitcher of sangria, and here we are...having a ball for ourselves."

"I thought you'd given up alcohol."

"There's alcohol in sangria? That's *right*. How *stupido* of me. How about you? I'll bet Noelle mixes strong drinks."

"Angela, I'm tired, let's call it a night."

"When will I see you?"

"When I get off the plane Thursday night," she said sharply.

"Don't be so *testy*! I *miss* you, that's all."

"Wonderful. Good night, Angela, I'm going to sleep." As Micki turned out the light a few minutes later, the phone rang.

"Now what's up?" Micki asked angrily. "Checking to see that I'm not still at Noelle's?"

"My friends have left, it's quiet here now. I'm calling to say I love you." Her voice was soft, her expression tender.

Micki pulled the sheet up over her shoulders. "You do?" she asked, pleased that Angela had called, though seconds ago she'd been furious with her. "Same here, you know that, don't you?"

"Yes. I'll meet you at the gate Thursday."

"Wonderful."

"Did you cheat on me tonight?"

"No," Micki said emphatically, "I didn't."

"And you're in your room by yourself?"

"I'm in *bed* by myself."

"Sweet dreams, then, Micki."

"You, too, love."

Micki hung up, sighed and turned over.

On the return flight, Micki was looking forward to seeing Angela again. Though she'd kept a full schedule in New York, when she stopped for an afternoon coffee break earlier in the day, she felt depressed by their separation. As she sat in the crowded restaurant, her life seemed tentative and empty without Angela. She hoped Angela would be on time to meet the plane.

Micki began the long walk toward the Arrivals gate, scanning the awaiting crowd for Angela. She didn't see her.

The overnight bag was heavy, her feet were swollen and sore, she felt crushed by the weight of her coat.

If not for Angela, she'd be going back to the peace and quiet of her empty apartment. What would she do with that peace and quiet? And how would she deal with the emptiness?

She scanned the crowd again, feeling anxious, now. Then she saw Angela hurrying her way. They waved to each other.

Angela was dressed casually in a leather jacket, jeans and boots. She took the bag from Micki, kissed her quickly, held her hand.

"You're home, Mama," she said happily.

"Yes...and what a life-saver you are tonight. I'm so bushed I'm not sure I'd have had the energy to even make it to the cab stand if you hadn't shown up."

"No chance of *that* happening. What was it? Bad trip? Bad flight? Or did you just miss me?"

Micki looked at Angela, then wrapped her arm around her waist. "I missed you, sweetheart, I missed you so damn much."

"Good, 'cause I sure missed you."

"God," Micki said, unlocking the door to the apartment, "am I glad to be home."

"Just sit down, kick off those high heels of yours and I'll treat you to the driest martini you've ever tasted."

"You? Mixing martinis? What's up?"

"Nothing's *up*, Micki. But you look as if you could use some tender loving care after a few days in that nasty city."

Angela brought Micki her drink and then sat down beside her. She kicked off her boots and reached down to take off Micki's shoes. Then she stood, unzipped her jeans and left them on the floor at her feet. She sat cross-legged on the sofa, facing Micki.

Angela leaned forward and kissed her. "Want another lemon peel?" she said softly.

"No." She couldn't stop looking at Angela. "I want you ...right here."

In one swift movement, Angela raised her black T-shirt over her head, threw it on the floor with her jeans.

"Just like this, right? Nice and comfy."

"Exactly," Micki replied.

"You really missed me?"

Micki's response was to take Angela in her arms.

"You've come home to good news, love. I've got a surprise for you."

"New York?" Micki asked. Fear of losing Angela shot through her body.

"Better. Guess where?"

"*Where?*"

"The Caribbean...St. Maarten."

"What sense does that make when you know it's only a matter of time before New York makes an offer?"

Angela pulled away, sat up. "I'm not talking about a *job*, I'm talking about an *assignment*. Eight wonderful days in paradise. We're doing a month long series on winter vacation spots and I really lucked out."

"You'll have a wonderful time." There was disappointment in Micki's voice at the prospect of another separation.

"I? I? Moi? Myself? No, my darling, *we* are going to the island of St. Maarten. You can take a week off, can't you? Will you come?"

"You couldn't keep me away," Micki said excitedly. "It's an island I've always wanted to visit."

"I'm glad neither one of us has been there before. It makes it more special."

Angela reached for Micki's hand and said, "Why don't we go into the other room? You look uncomfortable in all those clothes. I can just tell how much you want to relax."

Once in bed, Angela sprawled over Micki, teased her with her tongue, nuzzled her wherever she could, tasting her breasts, her nipples, the soft warm flesh of her shoulders. Now and then Micki stopped Angela, took her in her arms and kissed her, but then Angela wriggled free, wanting to play some more.

With her tongue, Angela stroked Micki's stomach, circled her navel, nipped her thighs, tiny red love marks suddenly appearing. She wove a circle of Micki's fine, blond pubic hair around her finger, bent down, kissed her gently.

Then abruptly, she sat up. "How many bathing suits shall we take?" she asked, her mind racing ahead to their holiday. "At least three, don't you think?"

Micki had grown used to sudden changes with Angela, but just at this moment, she hadn't been expecting one. She sat up, propped herself against a pillow. "If you really want to talk about swim wear now, three sounds about right. But I thought you were going there to work."

"There'll be some of that, sure...but why can't I wear a bikini when we're taping? It might help my career!"

"You and that career of yours are going to do just fine," Micki said, leaning back. Then she pulled Angela close to her. "I missed you so these past few days."

"You're home now," Angela replied, "that's all that matters." She kissed Micki hungrily, inviting her caresses.

Micki responded eagerly, holding small, firm breasts in her hands, her thumbs circling Angela's nipples, flesh becoming taut, color growing pinker, redder. With her thigh, Micki pushed Angela's legs apart, then slowly she made her way down Angela's body.

As they made love, Angela's soft urgings broke the silence of the night. Micki could taste the climax about to begin, and as those seconds came closer, were within the turning of an instant, Micki pulled away.

"Don't *stop*."

"I want to make it last for you," Micki whispered.

"It can't, Micki...take me....you'll drive me crazy if you don't," Angela pleaded.

Ever so slowly then, Micki increased the pressure of her love making until her pace matched Angela's frenzy. With Angela, now, sex was a ball of fire exploding in the night.

Micki continued caressing, demanding, urging her again and within seconds, Angela's passions were released once more. Micki held Angela close to stop her lovely body from trembling.

When Angela spoke, her voice was husky. "You didn't do this with her, did you?"

Micki whispered, "No, baby, no," and held Angela all the tighter.

"Don't ever cheat on me, Micki. You'll never get away with it. Never."

She kissed Micki passionately. "I could die having sex with you, Micki," she said urgently.

Then, like a cat would, Angela purred and curled up in her arms.

CHAPTER 10

The trip was scheduled for mid-October, and in the weeks before their departure, Angela did the necessary research on St. Maarten. She'd been told to divide her focus between the Dutch and the French sectors of the island and she enthusiastically investigated possible side trips that would make the feature a little different from the usual.

She and Micki pored over guidebooks and drew up an itinerary for their leisure time. But if the first day on the island was any indication, the only time they'd be alone was when they were in their hotel room, and from the beginning, there were interruptions even there.

Before they'd gotten settled, Jackie Woolf, an associate producer, burst into the room and insisted on knowing when Angela was going to go over the script for the next day.

"I'm bushed, Jackie," Angela said wearily. "I need some time to get over that flight. How long *were* we in the air?"

"We're on the ground now, Angie," she said crisply.

"I'd at least like to have some dinner--"

"Let's block the shots first, then the night is yours."

"Slave driver," Angela said peevishly.

"Not at all," Jackie answered abruptly. "We've got a hell of a tight schedule to follow this week, and I intend to make sure we don't lose a minute's time."

"I think a sudden rush of power has gone to that woman's brain," Angela exclaimed, after her producer had left. "I'm sorry, Micki, I'll be back as soon as I can. Maybe we'll try our luck at a casino tonight. Sound like fun?"

"Depends on when you show up," Micki said agreeably.

"At the studio, we can go through a script in a half hour or so. Now that I think of it, I don't even know what Madame Woolf has scheduled for tomorrow."

"Don't forget, you're here to work, not play," Micki replied, as she comfortably stretched out on the bed. "Pass me the papers; I'll catch up on the news while you're gone."

When Angela returned nearly two hours later, Micki was sitting outside on a small balcony overlooking Great Bay. Stars had begun to appear in the sky in the twilight of a long tropical evening.

"I know it took longer than I said it would," Angela apologized, "but I think that bitch has got it in for me."

"What happened?" Micki asked with concern.

"Everything that possibly could have...and none of the details would interest you." Angela's voice reflected her frustration. Then suddenly her mood changed, and with a clap of her hands and a bright smile she said, "Tomorrow's all set, and guess what? I should be through by nine thirty."

"What time do you *start?*"

"Jackie wants us on location by six. Think we can skip the night life tonight and grab a quick sandwich somewhere?

Micki laughed, "We'll do better than that. This island's a gourmet's delight!"

They decided on an Indonesian restaurant and after a leisurely dinner returned to the hotel, both of them now admitting to travel fatigue.

The next morning, true to her word, Angela was back at the hotel room by nine forty-five, with fresh croissants and coffee.

, If nothing else," she said, "Jackie Woolf sticks to her schedule. Tomorrow we begin at two in the afternoon and work until eight in the evening. But for this afternoon, Jackie has set up a working lunch for the crew. Want to join us?"

Micki smiled cheerfully, "Thanks, darling, but I don't think that's a good idea. I'll take in a few of the sights or just relax on the beach for a couple of hours."

"I'm jealous," Angela complained.

"You're here to work, remember? And how did Jackie put it? 'We've got a hell of a tight schedule this week.'"

" 'And I intend to make sure we don't lose a minute!' If we've heard that once, we've heard it a *dozen* times. Maybe she'll come up with some new buzz words tomorrow."

Still, as Angela had promised, once she returned from lunch, the rest of the day was theirs. They'd arranged to rent a car early that evening, but by the time they finally drove out of Philipsburg and up into the hills, night was falling. A panorama of lights glittering in warm clusters from various small settlements sparkled on the hillsides like tiny jewels and separated the wealth brought by the tourists from the poverty that obviously was part of existence for the local people.

As they drove by a group of huts, Micki observed Angela taking in the scene. "You can't judge the natives' standard of living by our own," she offered. "I'm sure their living conditions could...probably should...be improved, but I've seen greater poverty on other islands."

"Perhaps, but huts are huts, wouldn't you agree?"

Micki shifted gears, took a sharp turn, and said, "Yes."

They continued to drive up the steep hill to heights that neither poverty nor tourism had touched. Rounding another curve, they spotted a luxurious contemporary home set on a bluff overlooking the turquoise waters of the Caribbean.

"How would you like to live here?" Angela asked, taking Micki's hand.

"If we did, would you forget the huts below?" she questioned.

"No, I wouldn't, but this is just a daydream, Micki. I'm happy with you wherever we are, you know that." She leaned across, kissed Micki, and said, "Let's turn back soon. I don't want either one of us too tired for love tonight."

"We won't be, Angela," Micki replied, "I'll follow the next sign for town."

*****

The first half of the week passed quickly for Micki even though Angela's schedule became busier with each day. She was patient with the demands made on Angela's time and assured her that after all, she *was* working. Micki used the hours to her own advantage and she wasn't surprised that some of the best times she had she spent just doing nothing. She stepped on a scale Wednesday morning and found she'd gained three pounds. She smiled. The trip was agreeing with her, but she was concerned about Angela's increased irritability over not being able to blend work and play so easily, and the increasing friction that it was causing with her producer.

A catamaran sail to nearby St. Bart's island had been scheduled and Angela insisted that Micki come along. The crew would be returning that afternoon, but Micki and Angela had arranged to spend the night at a guest house and sail back early the following morning.

As they left their mooring and sailed out of the marina, Micki chose a starboard deck chair that, for the moment at least, seemed to provide the most shade and the best view. Brightly colored billowing sails from one of the other large catamarans skimming the brilliant blue waters caught Micki's attention. She reached for her camera, took several shots.

"Don't put that camera away," Angela called from the stern where the crew had assembled. "Look what's coming!"

Micki turned, waved to Angela and caught her breath at the sight of a half dozen sail boats following swiftly behind in the wake of their own vessel, the **Skylark.**

"I won't miss this," Micki said excitedly, focused the camera and took a series of shots.

It wasn't long before Angela was able to join her and, as was the style on the island, refreshments were soon offered to all. Fresh fruits and juices, chilled Dutch beers, French wines and cheeses, one tray after another was passed about.

The winds were favorable that morning and in less than two hours, the **Skylark** approached Gustavia's harbor on St. Bart's. After they docked, the crew clustered around Jackie, who went over the schedule for the day in her usual efficient manner. Then they all strolled leisurely toward the center of the tiny town where two cabs awaited them.

Micki still felt a bit uncomfortable mingling with the crew. They were pleasant enough, but she felt out of place and didn't quite know how to define her role where Angela was concerned. Micki said she'd just as soon spend the morning on her own, but Angela insisted she join them as the crew climbed into the cars, a vintage Renault and an old battered Volvo, for their tour of the island.

The driver, a heavy-set Frenchman in sun glasses and a dark beret, stopped the car at various scenic points. Clusters of houses clung to steep hillsides, their red tile roofs and white stucco exteriors sparkling in the morning sun.

The group's destination was a French restaurant on the far side of the island. Arrangements had been made for Angela to interview the English-speaking chef, and once the interview was completed, the crew would return to town and Micki and Angela would register at the Tamarinde Guest House.

The schedule for the following day wasn't due to begin until late afternoon, so Angela hadn't bothered to inform her producer that she wouldn't be returning with them.

As if they'd been friends for years, Angela linked her arm through Jackie's, smiled graciously, and said, "We're through now, aren't we?"

"Through shooting? Yes," she replied.

"And the **Skylark's** set to sail?"

"Whenever we're ready," Jackie answered crisply.

"Have a wonderful return trip! Micki and I decided we'd stay here overnight. It's a wonderful opportunity to explore another island...." She knew it took *chutzpah* to pull off a stunt like this, but what could Jackie say? How could she object?

Angela continued walking, her conversation a running commentary on all the reasons she was looking forward to her overnight stay on this island.

Jackie yanked her arm away from Angela's, stopped short, glared at her. "And what if we *need* you?" she asked irately.

"We've chartered a boat for seven tomorrow morning. You won't need me before *then*, will you?" Angela innocently inquired. "Our schedule doesn't begin until late afternoon."

She blew Jackie a kiss, and waved to the others. "See you, guys," she called out in a cheery voice, and then turned and walked towards Micki.

"I'm all yours," she said softly.

"I hope you know what you're doing," Micki replied in a cautionary tone of voice. "From the expression on Jackie's face, I'd say she's none too happy. Why didn't you tell her ahead of time?"

"I know her too well. If I had, she would have scheduled something for later. I want this day for us, darling, for us alone. Let's go check in."

Micki thought it was worth pursuing Angela's reasons for what she had just done, but when she tried to continue the discussion, Angela simply laughed it away.

"She doesn't *own* me, Micki," Angela said defensively.

"I know she doesn't," Micki replied.

As she watched her enjoyment at seeing the **Skylark** set sail, Micki realized how important it was to Angela that this day not be spoiled by anyone...by anything. Micki also knew Angela was trying to prove to her that they *could* combine a demanding career and their own relationship.

Later that afternoon, they rented a car, went in search of a private beach that had been described to them. They'd been assured that nothing on the island was difficult to find and that the beach was marked by a grove of lush fuschia bushes. As soon as Micki spotted these, she pulled the car in off the road, out of sight from other travelers.

As they walked, they marveled at the white, powdery sand beneath their feet, the crystal clear blue water. The tiny bay was surrounded by low hanging trees whose branches met the tide line and seemed to float along the surface of the sea.

Micki pointed to a small promontory jutting into the water. "I'll race you out to that point and back!"

"You think so?" Angela challenged, as they folded their shorts and shirts on large beach towels. "No way!"

Laughing, they ran down to the shore and into the tepid water. Micki began to swim in earnest, Angela lagged behind, diving for tropical fish, unusual shells. She surfaced only when she couldn't hold her breath any longer.

"Come on," Micki called, looking back. "*Race* me."

"I'll catch up."

But she didn't and Micki touched the tip of the point, turned over on her back and floated back to shore. She lay on the sand watching Angela swim her way.

"What held you up?" Micki asked.

"Parrot fish, four of them. They were beautiful."

Angela lay down beside her as waves from the incoming tide splashed against their feet.

Micki touched the tip of Angela's nose. "I won."

"I *let* you win."

Angela took Micki's hand and they closed their eyes, sounds from the sea and tropical birds surrounding them.

"This is paradise, isn't it?" Angela asked.

"I think so," Micki replied.

"Want to stay here? Forever?"

"You wouldn't tire of it?"

"Not this week," Angela said, laughing.

"And that's about your limit, isn't it?" Micki asked in a friendly voice.

"Are you complaining because I have a...streak of restlessness in me?"

"Not at all," Micki said, as she reflected on how quickly Angela grew bored, how often her focus shifted.

"Don't tell me you'd be content with living on one of the islands," Angela retorted.

"I wouldn't, you're right, but I think I'm more easily contented than you are."

"Give me a chance, Micki. I've yet to see so much of what you already know, what you've experienced--"

"You're right, Angela. I'm sorry. When I was your age, I had a thousand dreams...at least."

"*That's* where we're different...I have only one...you."

"That's all?" Micki asked skeptically.

"All right," Angela grudgingly conceded, "My career...but you're part of that. You know that, don't you?"

Micki smiled. "Let's swim a bit," she said, standing and reaching for Angela's hand.

They walked out into the water until it was waist high, then they turned over on their backs and floated, bobbing up and down, enjoying the warmth of the water, the hot, tropical sun.

Suddenly, Angela turned over, dived down, swam toward Micki who stood in the shoulder-high surf. Playfully, Angela swam between Micki's legs as if they were a tunnel. She surfaced, stood beside Micki, reached for her, held her close. They kissed, tasting the salty wetness in each other's mouths, and hand in hand strolled back to shore.

The two lovers lay on the sand as a foamy surf splashed gently against their legs, crept up to their thighs with the incoming tide. They moved back to their towels, lay close to each other, until Angela saw the first star and the promise of a new moon.

*****

They were reluctant to leave the next morning, but it was Micki who insisted they meet the charter as planned. Once back in their hotel, it wasn't more than a few minutes before there was a knock at the door and Jackie Woolf burst into the room.

"Where *were* you yesterday afternoon?   We checked *everywhere*...your guest house, restaurants, the tennis court--"

"I don't play tennis," Angela replied.

"That's not the *point*," Jackie said. "Didn't you get the message to call?"

"No," Angela said angrily, "I didn't!"

"We needed you and you were *nowhere* to be found," Jackie fumed. "Because of that, we lost a day's shooting and the segment you wanted on St. Bart's."

"What are you *talking* about? We finished, damn it."

"Unfortunately, the camera malfunctioned and the film was ruined--"

"Oh, no," Angela said, sitting on the bed.

"We had a spare camera, Angela, and plenty of film. If you'd been with us instead of off with your friend here, we could have returned and reshot the sequence."

"Jackie, I'm sorry."

"That's of no help right now. We've fallen behind schedule, lost a day's work. Sometime, Angela, you'll learn that if you want to stay in this field, you won't be able to *mix* business with pleasure. What made you think you could try?"

Angela didn't answer.

"You've got thirty minutes to get to the town square," Jackie continued.   "We'll do a fill-in segment on the fruit and vegetable market. But hurry, it looks like rain. I don't want to waste another day."

Angela slammed her bag against the door. "Whether she knows it or not, that woman is riding my case and I'm getting tired of it. Don't think I'm not going to raise the roof when we get back to Boston--"

"Can you blame her?" Micki asked gently.   "No one else brought a lover along."

"Lover? She doesn't know you're my lover."

"Don't kid yourself, but that's not the issue. No one else brought a friend, husband, wife...or lover. They came down here alone...to work."

"Haven't I been working?"

"You've also been playing, haven't you?" Micki prodded.

"So?" Angela barked defiantly.

"She's right, you can't mix the two. In any business. I should have had the sense to say no when you first told me about this trip. It wasn't a particularly smart idea for me to come along, was it?"

Angela shook her head in frustration. "Don't say that," she said angrily. She slammed her hand down on the table, split a fingernail. "Now look what I've done!" she exclaimed.

She darted into the bathroom, shut the door, called out, "Where the hell is my nail file?"

She rummaged through her makeup kit, grabbed the file, then reached into a zipper compartment for a small plastic bottle. She yanked out the cotton plug, shook a handful of amphetamines into her palm, carefully selected two, capped the bottle, tossed the pills down with a swallow of water. She looked at her reflection in the mirror, ran a brush through her glossy hair, picked up her nail file, and opened the bathroom door.

"Just what I need now...split nails," she exclaimed. Then she walked over to Micki, kissed her on the mouth, held her in a tight embrace.

"You're right," she whispered passionately, "I know you're right. Before I met you, I never would have thought of doing what we've done this week. But darling, it's been one of the best times I've ever had, and that--and you--makes it worth more than *anything* this business could offer me."

"You're going to have to make choices, Angela," Micki said decisively. "And soon."

"Meaning?"

"New York...the network job...it's bound to come."

"There's no choice there, Micki," Angela said with conviction. "We'll commute between the two cities. We won't be the first couple to do it, that's for sure."

"It's not going to be so easy," Micki said with concern.

There was a sharp rap at the door. "Hall," Jackie barked. "Now. We're waiting."

Angela smiled as she felt a sudden rush from the uppers. "Be right there," she called brightly.

"Don't keep them waiting," Micki cautioned. "The crew's got only so many hours before we all head back to Boston."

"Like the pretty woman sings, sweetheart, 'don't you worry 'bout a thing'," Angela said, kissing Micki goodbye. "And when the time comes, Micki, I'll make a choice...the right choice...for us. You can count on me for that."

After Angela left the room, Micki stepped out on the balcony. Something about Angela was bothering her, although she couldn't quite put her finger on it. But a few minutes later, when Angela and the crew emerged from the hotel lobby, the feeling disappeared, and Micki's only thoughts were that she hoped everything would go all right.

CHAPTER 11

Autumn's remaining weeks passed swiftly and soon the holiday season moved into high gear. Merchandise meetings and staff problems kept Micki at work more than she liked. Angela was busy as well, completing stories that often were lead-in features on the six o'clock news. She was putting the final touches on a gun control story when her agent, Tom Haskell, called to tell her the good news.

"How's your calendar look for the second week in February?" he asked cheerfully. Without waiting for a reply, he said, "Your interview with Pat Donovan's set! It's scheduled for Monday the ninth at eleven o'clock. Can you make it?"

"Channel Ten's Pat Donovan?" she asked excitedly.

"None other," he replied confidently. "I've been on the phone with his associate most of the afternoon. The Evening News has solid ratings, a steady audience, but Pat's looking for an experienced reporter to work on unusual stories that will attract a wider range of viewers. Are you interested?"

"Of course," she answered. "You know I am! But why wait until February? It seems so far off!"

"Pat doesn't want to make any changes until after the new year, Angela. Be patient. After all, this is quite a step for you."

"I wonder how many others are being considered," she said, trying to envision her competition.

"Just be prepared to do your best. I'll be in Boston later this month. We'll choose your strongest tapes. In the meantime, why don't you start reviewing them?"

As the conversation ended, she thought of calling Micki, then decided it would be more exciting to share the news when she arrived home that evening.

Angela had already decided that if she were offered a network job, she'd persuade Micki to come with her. She wasn't pleased with the notion of two domiciles and a commuting relationship. As she cleared papers from her desk, she began to fantasize about the apartment they'd have in Manhattan. Micki likes the Upper East Side, she told herself, that's where we'll look. She left the office, hurried to the apartment, arranged a large bouquet of fresh flowers in a vase, chilled a bottle of wine. She picked one of Micki's favorite Michael Feinstein tapes, turned on the music, and waited for her.

Micki's demeanor was calm as she listened to Angela describe the details of the conversation with her agent, but she knew that Angela was making assumptions about the future they'd need to discuss. For now, outwardly at least, she remained cool as Angela bubbled over with enthusiasm.

On Sunday afternoon, as Micki clipped a few dry flowers from the bouquet, Angela presented her with the help wanted section from *The New York Times.*

"If you start looking now," Angela began, "we'll be able to move down at the same time."

Micki smiled, dropped the paper on the coffee table, took Angela's hands in her own, and led her to the sofa. She sat back comfortably, encouraged Angela to do the same.

"I'm very happy for you, darling, you know that, don't you?" Micki asked softly, soothingly. "We're going to have to incorporate so many changes in our relationship, and it's not going to be easy. We haven't been together that long; we're still learning about each other, wouldn't you agree?"

"I've learned what I like, Mama," Angela said lightly.

"Be serious for a bit, we need to talk," Micki implored.

"Okay, let's work out the game plan. That's what *this* is all about," she said as she reached for the newspaper.

Micki took the paper, but placed it back on the table. As she spoke, her tone was firm. "I'm very comfortable at Hewitt's, I like my job. I'm not leaving Boston--"

"You know there are more opportunities in New York---"

"You're not listening," Micki insisted.

"I'm not losing you, Micki, not even for New York." Angela's eyes darkened with frustration, anger. "There's nothing to discuss! Either I have you *and* the network job or I stay here so that we're together."

"Angela, we are *together*, " Micki said patiently. "Your moving to New York won't change that, believe me. We'll work everything out, I promise you, only we have to start dealing with things."

As the weeks passed, Micki tried to initiate conversations about the prospective move, but Angela was quick to avoid anything other than the most superficial discussions. Micki suspected that for Angela, as long as the topic of separation wasn't seriously examined, it wasn't a reality. And Micki often admitted to herself that she was having her own share of problems in trying to accept what she felt was the inevitable. Work, however, demanded more time than ever, and for both of them, it became a convenient escape.

*****

Though Hewitt's was open until five o'clock on Friday, Christmas Eve, Micki left her office at noon. She stopped by the Advertising Department to wish Beverly Keating happy holidays, and wasn't surprised to see that she, too, was getting ready to leave.

"All finished?" Micki asked cheerfully.

Beverly laughed. "With work, yes, but I *still* haven't finished shopping. I'm hoping the store's deserted by now."

"No such luck," Micki responded. "When I walked across the floor a few minutes ago, the place was mobbed."

"Thanks for the good news," she said glumly, reaching for a bright red scarf which she draped over her shoulders.

"Why don't you drop by this weekend?" Micki inquired. "Angela and I don't have any special plans beyond enjoying a quiet holiday with each other."

"I might," Beverly replied, "if I make an early exit from my sister's place in Portland. That's where I'm heading after I finish shopping."

"Call when you get back," Micki urged. "Bring a friend with you if you like."

As Beverly slipped on her coat and picked up her bag, she smiled. "A friend? If I had someone special right now, I doubt I'd be heading north to Maine. The drive's bound to take close to three hours with all the holiday traffic." She groaned in mock dismay. "My sister and her husband have five kids! Can you imagine tomorrow morning?"

"You'll have fun," Micki replied, as she and Beverly left the office.

"I know...I wouldn't miss it for the world." She turned and hugged Micki warmly. "You and Angela have a special day," she said affectionately.

"You folks, too," Micki said, waving goodbye.

Micki took her time walking through the Common, stopped to listen to warmly bundled carolers gathered around the traditional nativity scene. Light snow was falling. She brushed wet flakes from her face as she continued home, the familiar words of "Silent Night, Holy Night" merging with incessantly shrill car horns from drivers frustrated by Tremont Street grid lock.

She crossed Charles Street, walked quickly through the Public Garden, and headed for her own apartment on Beacon Street. She checked for mail, took out a handful of Christmas cards, and pressed the buzzer twice so Angela, who wasn't scheduled to work over the holiday, would know she was on her way up.

She tried the door. Locked. Angela must be picking up last minutes presents, she thought, or the station had called her in, after all.

The only way she'd managed the weekend off was to offer to be on twenty-four hour call.

Micki's disappointment quickly changed when she unlocked the door and opened it to see Angela finishing the trimming of a tree that nearly touched the ten foot ceiling.

"Surprise," Angela cried with excitement. "How do you like it? All we need now is the star at the top and I've saved that for you."

"I wondered why you didn't answer the door, sweetheart," Micki said, reaching up to squeeze her hand, relieved that Angela was home.

"Don't you know you can't interrupt an *artiste* in the middle of a creation?" Angela replied as she looked down at Micki from the top rung of the stepladder. "Now what do you think? How does it look?"

The tree had been placed in front of the large picture window overlooking the Charles River. It was a lovely scene: tiny white tree lights, bright Christmas decorations, the tall Scotch pine, snow flakes hugging the window, and beyond that the city of Cambridge, its many lights glittering like stars for the holiday.

"It couldn't be lovelier," Micki said softly. "You've done a wonderful job."

"Thank *you*! And after you put the star in place," she said, hopping down to give Micki a hug and kiss, "all you have to do is to sit back and enjoy some of my eggnog. It is *delicious*!"

Later in the afternoon, Micki looked once more at the many Christmas cards she and Angela had received. She smiled at Lana and Ruth's greeting which featured a pair of fluffy angora kittens peering out of a bright red stocking. Noelle and Jessie's card depicted Renaissance musicians playing lutes and horns. She affectionately reread notes from various friends and then turned to family cards which had been carefully arranged on the marble mantel. Her son, Mark, had written of a new job; he promised to call on Christmas. In Pittsburgh, Micki's sister Kathleen had plans for the traditional Christmas buffet after midnight mass. Won't you join us? she'd written. Micki sighed wistfully. *Too bad we can't be everywhere at once*, she thought, *at least once a year*. She glanced once more at Angela's cards: her father's affectionate greeting, holiday joy and love from her sister Teresa, cards from her brother, several aunts and uncles, her grandmother.

Micki smiled with contentment, as once more she admired the tree, the sight of brightly wrapped gifts surrounding it, and the pleasant, familiar sounds of holiday music playing softly in the background.

It was a quiet, peaceful evening for both of them, and when the Arlington Street church bells chimed a carol at the midnight hour, Micki and Angela happily wished each other a very Merry Christmas.

*****

Micki was pleased that they'd both managed to get the weekend off, and she suggested spending the Sunday after Christmas at the Museum of Fine Arts.

"We can see the French Impressionists collection, have a leisurely lunch, then take in a bit of the Boston Printmakers show, how's that strike you?" Micki inquired pleasantly.

"Wonderful," Angela replied. "Give me twenty minutes to shower and dress and I'll be ready."

Micki zipped the fly front of her grey slacks, pulled on a navy wool sweater, looked for her brush and realized she'd left it in the bathroom.

"Want me to dry you off?" she called, knowing that the shower had been turned off a few minutes earlier.

As she opened the door, she was shocked to see Angela furtively reach for a pill bottle she'd dropped.

"What are those?" Micki asked, watching Angela scoop up several pills which had scattered across the floor.

"Do you always have to give me the third degree?" she asked angrily. "I've got a headache, that's all!"

"Why didn't you tell me? We don't have to go out this afternoon," Micki replied. "And besides, the aspirin are in the medicine cabinet, you know that. What *are* those pills? What are you taking now?"

"You really want to know? I get the blues the day after Christmas, always have. There's nothing unusual about that, is there? These harmless little pick-me-ups always do the trick, Micki. You should try a couple yourself instead of being so goddamned serious about everything. Lighten up, baby, we're moving into a new *year* next week, and I don't want to feel like I'm being spied on all the time." Angela wrapped her arms around Micki, smiled, kissed her on the lips. "Come on," she pleaded, "I'm a big girl...and you can take my word for it, these are *not* drugs."

"What are they then?" Micki asked, pulling back.

"Joy gems," Angela laughed, "tiny gems of joy."

"These lies have got to stop!" Micki said, her voice tense with anger and frustration. "I'm no expert on drugs and I doubt that you are either, but our relationship, our future, your *career* are all going to fall apart unless you resolve this. You're on the edge too much of the time...hanging from the edge. And you have me there with you! It's not what I want for either one of us. Angela, you've got to face this problem---"

"You're calling it a *problem*, I'm not! Do you think I should talk to a shrink about a few pills, a line of coke once in a while, is that it? Or about what I did when I was five years old? Why should I?" she shouted angrily.

"Why don't you look in the mirror for a change?" she continued. "Tell me how you rationalize your love of fine wine! Social drinking, right? No problem...but what about your smoking? Tobacco is one of the most *addictive* drugs...."

Micki watched carefully as her monologue continued, then she walked into the living room, sat down, stared out across the Charles River. When the phone rang a few minutes later, she felt nothing more than a dull sense of relief as Angela responded to the request from Channel 8 that she fill in this evening for the usual anchor who'd come down with bronchitis.

Before Angela left for the TV studio, she tried to apologize for having to work, and for the argument they'd had.

"New Year's Eve we'll make our resolutions, Micki," she said, wrapping her arms around Micki, holding her in a close embrace. "Whatever you want me to do, I will...and vice versa...all right?"

"I'm not joking with you," Micki said with clear determination. "I think you should talk to someone. This dependence on drugs has *got* to end, I really mean it."

"I know you do," Angela said soberly, realizing that Micki meant what she said. "But I'll handle things myself, I promise you. Trust me," she pleaded.

When Beverly Keating phoned a short while later, Micki knew she wasn't in the mood to entertain.

"Angela's been called in to work," she explained. "What if we all get together some evening during the week?"

"That's fine," Bev responded, "but how about you? In the mood for a walk along the Charles? We could stop for coffee and pastry at the Cafe Verona on our way back."

Micki looked out at the bright blue winter sky, felt the warmth of the sun streaming in through the large picture windows of her apartment, agreed with Bev that it was the ideal day for a bit of exercise. Their walk along the bank of the river took them as far west as the Mass. Ave. bridge, where they decided to stroll over to Newbury Street, window shopping on their way to the cafe.

It wasn't until they were seated at the small window table overlooking the busy street that the conversation changed from small talk to what had been on Micki's mind all along. She began by speaking candidly about the tensions surrounding Angela's situation at the station.

"I just *wish* the decision would be made, Bev, it's getting to be hell for her," she said bluntly.

"And rough on the two of you, I take it," Beverly commented. "You seem angry yourself, Micki. What about? Are *you* afraid of the move? Tell her then, ask her to postpone the change."

"I don't want to hold her back...I don't want to lose her either..." Her voice trailed off as she gazed across the room, then she turned to Beverly, smiled tensely.

"You know," she continued, "sometimes when I watch her, I get the greatest satisfaction out of turning the TV off while she's in the middle of a sentence."

"You're furious she's leaving, aren't you?" Bev asked, watching Micki's eyes to see if her expression conveyed the same frustration as her words.

Micki evaded her glance by looking out into the street, ignoring Beverly's question as she played with the tips of faded flowers in a blue glass vase. In truth, she felt they *could* handle any problems connected with Angela's moving to New York, even though it would be far from ideal. Countless couples were separated by distance today, she thought. They could cope with being apart...it was the other problem...the other situation that was so hard for Micki to even begin to discuss.

"I don't mean to pry," Bev said gently, "but you seem lost in *deep* thoughts. *Is* something else troubling you?"

Micki hesitated, wanting to be careful in what she said, yet at the same time finally admitting to herself that she needed to share this problem with *someone*. "Angela's aura, the excitement she creates, her highs...and her lows...don't occur on their own, Bev. For months, I've rationalized her mood swings, tried to overlook them, told myself she's a complicated woman, but *finally* I'm admitting what I've seen with my own eyes. She's on...pills...uppers, for the most part, I think."

"She's addicted to these?" Beverly asked, her expression revealing surprise.

"*NO*, no, I'm sure she's not," Micki protested, wanting to believe Angela's claims about herself. "But she refuses to see where these...pills can lead."

"*Does* she take anything else?" Bev inquired.

"You've got to keep this between us," Micki confided. "She's experimented with coke...I don't think very often...but who knows what else she takes? I think Angela needs to see someone, but she denies that there's a problem. Half the time she convinces *me* there isn't..." Micki shrugged her shoulders as her words trailed off into silence.

Bev reached across the table for Micki's hand. "And who's denying now? You know I'm here for you, don't you, Micki?" she asked entreatingly. "Regardless of what Angela does about *her* problem, *you* need to see someone. Try to get some understanding about why it took you so long to admit any of this--"

"I'm too old to be dabbling in shrinks," she retorted. "I've made it *this* far without anyone's help...you know I had *years* of hard times...problems during the marriage, after the divorce. That's when I probably *should* have gotten help, but I didn't! Somehow, I got through it myself, and I'll get through this, too," she said vehemently.

"Micki," Bev implored, "these aren't *your* rough times...they're Angela's. You don't...you can't...understand them."

"But I *live* them," she said with quiet anger.

"I can see that," Beverly responded.

From a small notebook, she wrote down a name and phone number, tore out the sheet, passed it across the table.

"Here's the phone number of a lesbian therapist, Micki, Dr. Irene Trager. She's terrific. Call her."

Micki's fingers tapped the paper quickly, nervously. "I'm not sure about this," she said reluctantly.

"I know," Beverly replied. "Take it anyway."

Micki slipped the sheet of paper into her pocket, touched the faded flowers once more. She watched as petals clinging to her fingertips dropped to the white linen tablecloth.

*****

Early morning snow had turned to slush and Micki felt depressed knowing that the icy water had already seeped through the soles of her boots. Why was it next to impossible to make a waterproof boot, she thought glumly.

On a day as bleak as this one, nothing was grayer than the Fens. Dating to the early 1900's, this section of Boston consisted, for the most part, of gray granite and yellow brick buildings. They had always struck Micki as an anachronism in a city whose architecture was more typically the red brick which characterized town and row houses everywhere from Beacon Hill to the South End.

The street number she was looking for came up too fast for Micki's liking and she almost decided not to ring the bell. She knew, though, that Beverly had been right and that she *did* need to talk to someone.

The waiting room was simply furnished with chairs, small tables displaying the usual array of magazines, and lamps dimly lighted. Micki stared at the large, bold face card tacked to the faded tan wall that expressed thanks for not smoking. She looked at her watch and waited nervously for her appointment.

Punctually at ten o'clock, one of three inner doors opened and Dr. Irene Trager entered the room. Thick, dark eyebrows were a contrast to her hazel eyes, and light brown hair which was brushed casually back from her face. She wore a magenta sweater, a grey skirt flecked with threads of blue, and boots, which, by Micki's quick appraisal, did appear to be water proof. She smiled warmly, extended her hand in greeting, and invited Micki to accompany her into the office.

Micki stood awkwardly beside a small teak desk until Dr. Trager gestured toward an arrangement of furniture which included a sofa and three chairs. As she sat down, Dr. Trager took the chair next to hers.

"Micki," she said, her voice reflecting concern, "how can I help you?"

Minutes passed as Micki contemplated how to begin. She studied the therapist's face, relieved that she wasn't as young as she feared she might be. Responding to an expression of trust which she saw in her eyes, Micki began to talk about the last few months with Angela and about recent events which had brought her to this office.

When the hour was drawing to a close, Dr. Trager said, "A problem involving a couple as committed as you and Angela seem to be is best treated by both partners entering into therapy. I'd like Angela to join you next week--"

"That won't happen," Micki interrupted. "She's adamant about even the *suggestion* that she has a problem."

"But you *do* feel," she said, her voice reflecting understanding, "that she has a drug problem."

"I honestly don't know, Dr. Trager. She's like a person who goes to a party and doesn't drink until the last half hour, then has three or four quick ones for the road.

"When she wants to get across the street," Micki continued, "she just shoots out, not looking either way, and I rush after her."

"You see her behavior as destructive," the therapist said slowly, deliberately, "yet you seem to be saying that by being drawn into it, you're a part of it."

"Something like that," Micki conceded.

"One thing to keep in mind," she explained, "is that there are as many shades to addiction as colors in a rainbow. And whether the substance involves drugs, alcohol or both, what we've known for a long time is that often in a relationship such as yours, one partner *enables* the other to continue the dependence. That may *not* be the case here, but we need to explore other issues, other questions.

"It will take time," she said, concluding their conversation, "but I think I can help you to understand your part in what has occurred."

Micki nodded assent, grateful for Dr. Trager's optimism, relieved that she'd finally begun to share what she now saw as a burden.

CHAPTER 12

As the weeks passed, Beverly became a loyal and much needed confidant for Micki. When Angela worked late or was out of town on a story, more often than not, Micki called Beverly. It turned out they needed each other.

Beverly had begun to talk to Micki about her last relationship, a four year affair that had ended several months ago. The woman had been an intern at Boston City Hospital, and when she decided to take a position on the west coast, she told Beverly that although she loved her, it was time for them to explore new territories, to free each other, to move on. Beverly still felt the pain of rejection.

One night, Micki suggested that Beverly stop off at the Stardust Cafe, a women's bar in Cambridge, where she'd agreed to meet Angela later. They found an empty table in a quiet nook and as they sat down, Beverly smiled at Micki.

"What has you in such a good mood?" Micki asked.

"I feel very positive about our getting to know each other the way we have these past several weeks," Beverly replied.

"We've become good buddies, I agree."

"I've come to the conclusion," Beverly continued, "that there's something *nice* about middle-age. It's *comforting* to have settled into who you are." She laughed. "I must be getting Jennifer out of my system...finally. Whatever it is, I feel a great sense of relief. I don't have to *hustle* anymore...for anything, for anyone. Someone special will enter my life again someday. If not, I can make it on my own.

After all these years, Micki, we just *are*. The world can take us or leave us 'cause I've decided we ain't gonna change," she concluded.

"Guess we're not," Micki agreed. She focused on a young woman sitting alone at the bar, leafing through the pages of a newspaper.

"Looks like Angela, doesn't she?" Beverly asked.

"A little, perhaps."

"She's your type. That's why Angela's perfect for you. I could have drawn a sketch of her before you two even met."

"How do you know so much about me?" Micki inquired.

"Intuition."

"And what's your type?"

"Tall, blonde, successful," Beverly said, pronouncing each word slowly.

"I'll take a few of those myself," Micki said jokingly.

It didn't occur to Micki that Beverly was talking about her. After all, they were pals.

Beverly didn't see herself as having designs on Micki, nor did she wish her bad times with Angela, but she felt they were coming. She'd already decided that when they did, if Micki was interested, she'd be there for her.

Micki sipped the drink slowly. As she looked around the room at the young women who'd gathered, she felt exposed, vulnerable. Without Angela, she was a middle-aged woman, alone.

She was having difficulty admitting even to herself that she was afraid of losing Angela. She had talked about it with Dr. Trager, though, she mused, realizing how much she'd come to rely on their sessions over these past six weeks.

Insights gleaned sometimes from nothing more than broken sentences, stumbling feelings surprised her. Insecurities surfaced, not only about Angela's dependence on drugs, but her own concerns...and age was one of them. She'd begun to feel that a time would come when the difference in their ages would act against her, though Angela denied that it would ever be a problem.

And although Angela was obsessed with her now, Micki knew that obsessions, once fully satisfied, seek new and different subjects to complete identical desires.

Micki tried to remember what Dr. Trager had asked her the other day. She'd been talking about herself...about how difficult it was to admit that her marriage had failed, that she'd lost her child...what was it Dr. Trager had said?

"Do you find it easier to focus on Angela's needs than experience the pain you still must feel?" she had asked. "Are you evading crucial issues, still unresolved, concerning your *own* life?"

Micki remembered being confused by the question, and as she contemplated this, an ebullient Angela sat down beside her.

"Hi, darlin'," she said lovingly. "And Beverly, how are *you*? Micki, you didn't tell me our little tete-a-tete was going to be a threesome. What fun!"

Angela was like a top that evening, spinning out across the floor for brief conversations with familiar faces, then hurrying back to Micki to touch base before taking off again.

Bev noticed Micki's ring, complimented her on it, as she ran her hand across the sapphire set in diamonds.

"Isn't it beautiful," Micki asked. "Angela's Christmas present; I adore it." Micki shook her head in wonderment. "It still strikes me as...strange," she said, struggling for the words, "to be having the love affair of my life *now*. Weren't we always taught that passion was for the young?"

Beverly laughed. "I don't think you and I attended the same schools where love's concerned, Micki. Consider yourself lucky and don't question good fortune," she concluded. She touched Micki's hand once more, running her fingers lightly over the ring. "Angela has beautiful taste, if that ring's an example of it."

"An example of what?" Angela asked piercingly, stepping in between the two.

"The giver of wonderful gifts," Bev said in a friendly voice. "I was admiring your friend's ring--"

"My friend? She's my lover, my woman, my wife."

"Of course, darling, don't get *nervous*. That's exactly what I meant."

"Oh, buzz off," Angela said, not amused. "I wouldn't have bothered to come here, Micki, if I'd known you two were getting together!"

Beverly looked at Micki, who was obviously embarrassed at Angela's outburst, then she turned to Angela. "Has anyone ever told you how rude you are?" she asked sharply.

"Don't put the moves on my lover--"

Bev stood up, ignoring Angela.

"I think it's time for me to go," she said to Micki.

"I'm sorry about this," Micki apologized, "I really am. Perhaps it's just been too long a day. I'll talk to you tomorrow, Beverly."

"How could you let her talk that way to me?" Angela demanded, as Bev walked toward the door.

"Talk that way to *you*?" Micki exclaimed. "You're the one who was out of order."

"Really?"

"Don't be ridiculous, Angela."

"I know you cheat on me."

Micki looked at her in disbelief.

"You do, don't you?" Angela persisted.

Micki chose her words carefully. "You don't know what you're talking about. Let's get out of here before--"

Angela's drink hit Micki's face before she had a chance to realize what had happened. Alcohol burned her eyes as she blinked back tears of shock.

Quickly, the bartender stepped around the bar, stood next to Micki, and began to dry her face with a clean bar towel. Angela snatched the cloth from her.

"Get out," Angela snapped. "Who asked you to butt in?"

The woman held her ground, and when she spoke her voice was shaking with anger. "This is *my* bar! You're the one who's getting out...now...right now. Get *out* of my bar."

"Don't you ever do anything like that to me again," Micki said to Angela, her voice low, even, angry.

"She was on the make--"

"Shut up! Beverly's my *friend*! But what about *you*? You've been buzzing around this place since you walked in. Who do you think you *are*? What are you on now?"

Angela's eyes questioned her, then filled with tears. "Nothing," she protested, "I swear to you."

"I'm getting out of here," Micki said. "Alone."

"I want to come with you."

"No."

"Micki, please don't send me away. I'm coming with you."

Micki stood up, brushed the damp sleeve of her jacket, looked critically at Angela. "Let's get a cab," she said quietly.

Out on the street, Angela clutched Micki's arm, pulled her into the cab she flagged down, and gave the driver their address. Once inside the apartment, Micki leaned wearily against the door. Angela rushed at her, began to pound her shoulders.

"You cheat. You cheat. I know you do," she screamed.

"What put *this* idea into your head?" Micki demanded.

Angela pounded even harder in response to the question. Micki tried to protect herself by folding her arms in front of her body, then she tried to reach out to hold her, to calm her, but Angela pulled away, her hysteria growing.

Finally, as much to still Angela as to protect herself, Micki slapped her across the side of the face.

Then she turned away, sat down on the bed, buried her head in her hands, began sobbing. Angela knelt beside her. She lay her head on Micki's lap and cried. Micki held Angela then and comforted her.

"What is happening to us?" Micki finally asked.

"I'm so in love with you, Micki. I can't stand the thought of you being with anyone else."

"Angela, sit up here beside me. Stop crying or I'll start again myself."

She wiped the tears from Angela's cheek and kissed her lips. "Angela, let's slow down, the pressure's too much. We've got to *help* each other."

"I'll be good, I promise I will." The words were spoken in the voice of a child.

"You're not listening to me. We're pressured by everything--my job, the long hours, the traveling, the drugs you take, the network job, your distrust of me. The tension is unbearable.

"I've never cheated on you, I've never even thought of it! I'm in love with you! I want you to get this job. I want you to succeed at everything you desire, but Angela, I'm also afraid of losing you. Can't you see that? I've tried talking about it with you, but you ignore me, avoid the subject."

"I'll love you always, Micki--"

"We're going to need to trust each other--and ourselves-- or we won't be able to go on. I've told you how helpful Dr. Trager's been to me. Angela, I want you in therapy *with* me, give it a *chance*...at least talk to Dr. Trager!

"You'll have the world right in the palms of your hands one of these days...if you try to take care of things. But you've got to start facing some of these problems. Angela, it terrifies me that all of this might fall apart...that we might lose each other...that we might not be together."

Even now, Angela ignored Micki's pleas as she continued professing her love. When they finally went to bed, they clung to each other, each of them fearing to let the other one go.

CHAPTER 13

A peace followed the episode at the bar, though Angela was still adamantly opposed to joining Micki in therapy. Dr. Trager assured Micki that resistance to therapy was not uncommon and that often it took considerable time to overcome. What was important, she had said, was that Micki not take on the responsibility for Angela's decision.

In a phone conversation, Tom Haskell informed Angela that although the network still wanted to interview her, two of the news producers wanted to see what she was capable of doing in Boston over the next few months.

Angela had asked Micki if she thought this was a stalling technique. Why were they hesitating now? They had enough tapes of her broadcasts to know what her strengths and weaknesses were. What was behind the delay?

Though she was disappointed by this current decision, Angela was determined to work all the harder. When she was assigned a three part story on gun control, she told Micki she was sure that these pieces would do it for her.

Gun control and reform legislation were perennial topics for the station at least once a year. They'd decided to feature it now because of the recent deaths of two young boys who'd found a loaded semi-automatic shotgun in a barn near their homes in Holliston.

Angela's producer began to schedule a week of interviews for her with everyone from the Governor of the state to the mother of one of the boys. Out of these interviews would come a powerful story calling, once again, for the state to enact effective legislation.

While Angela went over scripts from previous stories on the subject, read background material from the Reference and Research Department, Micki asked her if she wasn't becoming too involved with the story.

"I've *got* to be involved. How else can I show them how really good I am?" she'd asked.

Because she was sympathetic to the pressure Angela was under, Micki decided not to argue for objectivity.

When she arrived home the following night, Micki saw the revolver on the coffee table as soon as she stepped into the living room. Angela, obviously agitated, disturbed, picked up the gun, waved it in the air.

"Where did you get *this*?" Angela cried.

"It's loaded, Angela, give it to me," Micki said evenly as she reached for the weapon.

"A loaded revolver?" she exclaimed. "Why? I've been working on this story for over a week and all that time we've had a gun in our own home--"

"It was in my closet, how'd you ever find it? What were you doing in there?" Micki inquired.

"Looking for a blanket...I was chilly, felt like curling up on the sofa while I worked."

Micki's expression was skeptical. Angela knew that extra blankets were stored in the linen closet in the hall.

"I'll be relieved when you finish this story. Let me put the gun away," Micki said calmly.

She took the revolver from Angela's hand and carefully placed it where it had been, at the rear of the top closet shelf. There was a general disorder in the closet, but Micki didn't comment on it when she returned to the living room.

"Now that it's safely out of the way, I'll explain," she began. "I've had the gun for years...since Guy and I were married. He bought it for me, for protection, after we'd had a run of break-ins in the neighborhood. I'd almost forgotten it was here. Funny, I never would have thought about it, if you hadn't been looking for...what?...a blanket?"

"Micki, get rid of the gun," Angela said sharply.

Micki shook her head, "This is my business."

"Then take the shells out," she responded quickly.

"I'm going to keep it as it is. No more talk about guns, okay? Let's try to ease up a little," Micki entreated. "We've both been working too hard, you especially."

"Accidents happen with guns every day, Micki. I don't have to be working on a story for us to know that."

"No accident will happen here," she assured her.

"I know what I'm talking about," Angela insisted. "We had guns in our house, too...my father's guns...souvenirs from the Bay of Pigs. I came home from school one day, I must have been about ten years old, and found my brother and sister playing war. With real guns!

"Papa had gone down to the basement to repair a water heater and had left his keys behind. Tommy wasn't even seven years old then, but he'd always been curious about the gun cabinet and couldn't resist unlocking it. Somehow, Papa had neglected to take the cartridges out of the weapon Tommy had in his hands. Tommy knew he shouldn't even have touched the keys, but he was excited, started running around the room, with both hands squeezed the trigger, and Teresa was wounded...in the shoulder. Blood was gushing everywhere, Teresa was crying, Tommy was terrified. Just then my father returned, and luckily, when Teresa was rushed to the hospital, it turned out to be little more than a flesh wound. But she could have been killed...and I know I would have felt that it was my fault."

"Now I understand why you're so involved with the story, but take it easy, slow down. Remember how?"

Angela smiled. "Yes. And don't be angry with me for exploding."

"I'm not," Micki said with careful deliberation. Then, wanting to change the subject, she asked, "Why don't we take in a movie? This is a good night to tune out and watch someone else's problems."

"I can't, love. This has to be perfect for tomorrow."

"How about dinner then? Let's walk over to Beacon Hill."

"Sure," Angela said agreeably, "that shouldn't take too much time."

"And then you can tell me what you were really looking for in that closet," Micki replied.

*****

The following week, Angela was sent to New Hampshire to cover a protest at the Seabrook Nuclear Power Plant. A conflict that had been brewing for months was about to erupt and protestors from all over New England lined the streets and roads leading to the plant.

Beverly had invited Micki over to her Commonwealth Avenue condo for a light supper Thursday evening, and as she set the table, she watched Angela's coverage of the story. She was impressed.

She expected Micki to arrive shortly after the news as they lived within blocks of each other, and before long the doorbell did ring. Beverly pressed the buzzer admitting Micki, who was dressed casually in worn levis, and a soft blue sweat shirt.

She handed Beverly a small white box containing French pastries, and for much of the time that Beverly assembled the meal, she sat quietly sipping coffee.

Micki had almost driven up to Seabrook the night before, but decided against it when she remembered the problems which had occurred for Angela on St. Maarten. She'd contented herself with waiting for Angela's phone call. It came a few minutes after her live broadcast had ended.

"How am I coming across?" she'd asked.

"Terrific, really fine, Angela. How long do you think the protest will last?"

"Some of these people look as if they're here to stay, it's hard to tell. I'm on their side--"

"Of course."

"Can you tell?"

"No, you seem impartial. Your reporting's objective--"

"Well, I'm *not*. There are real problems up here that might not surface until next week--"

"You're not coming back till next week?" Micki asked, in an aching voice.

The separations from Angela were harder than she ever admitted to Angela. She couldn't bear being alone for too long now, either.

"Like hell," Angela replied emphatically. "I'll be back as scheduled. Tomorrow. And I want breakfast in bed Saturday morning."

Micki smiled. "You'll have it."

"Can't wait to see you--I've got to go, love. There's a brain-storming session going on that I'm already late for."

"Miss you," Micki had said. But Angela had already hung up.

"You look as if you're lost in outer space," Beverly said, offering a plate of cheese and French bread. "Anything the matter?"

"Nothing that I'm not going to have to get used to more and more," she said pensively. "With Angela out of town so much of the time, I seem to be floating in limbo. About the only thing I can count on during the week is the hour I spend with Dr. Trager."

"Things are getting tough for you, aren't they, Micki?"

"There's more than enough pressure, that's for sure, but I'm glad I've begun therapy. I spend most of the sessions spewing out past hurts...I can't believe I have that much anger stored up in me. And it seems that it's only incidentally that I begin to talk about Angela. It's such a slow process, Bev, and I don't really know where it's headed."

"Do you feel guilty about going alone?" Bev asked.

"Not at all," Micki said laughingly. "Where else could I get the undivided attention of someone an hour at a stretch?"

"And is that all it is?"

"No, I'm being cruel. I wonder why? Dr. Trager's comments are helpful, her insights amaze me...I feel a warm, nurturing closeness with her."

"Does she say anything about Angela?"

"Not too much...though this past week, she asked me if Angela had given any more thought to therapy. Angela *refuses* to discuss it, gets angry if I try to tell her what went on during the sessions... sometimes I think she's even jealous of Dr. Trager," Micki responded.

"Competition," Beverly smiled.

"Maybe," Micki conceded.

Conversation turned to lighter subjects as Bev served dinner. Micki felt herself relaxing, unwinding, and it wasn't until nearly midnight that she walked back to her own apartment. Before going to bed, she unplugged the phone, something she often did when she was exceptionally tired, and within minutes she was sound asleep.

Before taking a shower the next morning, Micki plugged the phone jack back in, and when the phone rang a few minutes later, she had a good idea who it was.

"Good morning, love," she said, "I've been expecting you to call."

"Where *were* you all night?" Angela demanded. "I tried calling until four-thirty this morning. I was going to take a studio van and drive back to see if you were all right, but I knew I'd fall asleep at the wheel. I called you a dozen times, afraid you'd been hurt--"

"No, no, I was so tired last night, I just unplugged the phone and went to sleep. From the sounds of things up there, I thought you'd be at your brain-storming session most of the night."

"Well, I was--"

"I knew it," Micki interrupted.

"But I wanted to *talk* to you. Why didn't you tell me you were going to unplug the phone? You know I can't stand it when you do that."

"I'm so bushed these days, baby."

"And you think I'm not?"

Micki could hear the tiredness in Angela's voice. "I know you are," she said sympathetically. "Can't you get some sleep now?"

"If I only could. We're leaving for the site right now. But I'm coming back today with the first crew that drives out of here. And I'm going straight to bed. Can't you take the day off?"

"I've got an eleven-thirty meeting," Micki answered.

"So you weren't out prowling the streets last night?"

"No," she answered emphatically.

"And you weren't having a tete-a-tete with some other woman?"

"No," she said, "I had dinner with Beverly, came back here and fell asleep."

"Isn't that something?" Angela said brightly. "There I was worried sick about you. That's just not fair!"

"I'll be home as soon as I can today, how's that?"

"Wonderful! You know," Angela continued, "sometimes I think that Beverly's sharpening her eye teeth for you--"

"Don't be ridiculous," Micki said flatly.

"Let her try and she'll find I've been sharpening my claws." She laughed and then spoke in a bubbly, exuberant voice. "If Gary hadn't been up here with one of the camera crews, I *would* have driven back. He convinced me I'd probably kill myself on the highway. Then he said I had to control what he describes as my 'strange behavior'. How about that? You don't think I'm strange, do you love?"

"No, but I'm glad Gary stopped you. Give him a big hug and tell him I said thanks, will you?"

"Whatever you say, Mama!"

CHAPTER 14

Shortly after she arrived at work on the first Monday in May, Angela received the call that she was to meet with the News Director of Channel 10 that Friday morning at eleven.

Excited and nervous as she admitted she was, she told Micki that she'd decided to take the early morning shuttle to New York out of Logan Airport, rather than fly down the night before.

"I'd like it if you could come along," she said to Micki Thursday evening as she looked yet one more time at the outfit she'd chosen. "Couldn't you?"

Micki's tone was assuring. "Tom Haskell will be with you, he'll calm your nerves."

"Haskell? He wants his fifteen per cent, he doesn't care about my...state of being," she said dramatically. "Besides, he's convinced it's a sure thing. He told me that all I've got to do is get through this interview! Think it'll be that easy?"

"Why would they bring you this far to say no?"

"I don't know. Lately I've had this nagging feeling that there's something wrong about it, that maybe it wasn't meant to be. I just wish we had something lined up in New York for you, too."

She smiled at Micki, picked up a sleek black leather pump, brushed away a fleck of dust. She put the shoes beneath a suit which she'd hung on the outside of the closet door.

"Think I'll look all right in this? Is the blouse the right shade? Not too dull, is it?"

Angela had chosen a cream silk blouse to wear with the slate grey designer suit she'd bought on Newbury Street.

"What about a brighter tone to contrast--"

"No, I want to look successful...as if I already have everything that's going to come with the territory. I want a subdued... sophisticated image."

She slipped on the heels and pranced around the room playfully.

"Then I'd say you have it," Micki replied with certainty.

"Right now, I'm sure everything's going to work out, Micki...then other times, when I'm alone, I panic, I--"

"No panicking allowed tonight. And when you get back here with that contract signed, sealed and delivered, we are going to celebrate. I'll make reservations for dinner Saturday night. How does eight sound?"

"We'll take our time, enjoy every moment. For this, Micki, we deserve the Ritz."

"I'd say so," Micki agreed.

"Maybe I'll catch a late flight tomorrow night. I'll be too wound up to sleep, so I might as well come back here--"

"Angela," Micki cautioned, "you'll have a full day at the studio tomorrow; I'm sure there are plans for dinner--"

"Yes, but it's only with two *associate* producers. Donovan's the man I'm flying down to see and we're having lunch." She sat on the edge of the bed, took her shoes off, carefully placed them by the bedside table.

"Take the evening *with* the day, Angela, enjoy it," Micki said, joining her on the bed, putting an arm around her. She smiled, kissed Angela affectionately, and as lightly as she could, said, "What do you say we invest in airlines stock? Between the two of us, we'll be flying back and forth often enough to buy our own plane."

Angela smiled wistfully. "You don't think I should cancel out?"

"Be serious! Tomorrow morning, you're going to *look* like a million dollars and by tomorrow night, you'll feel you're worth that much. Who would turn that down?"

Angela had no answer, but she took Micki's hand and held it tightly in her own.

The next morning, Micki drove Angela to Logan Airport. They arrived early, with plenty of time to spare, yet Angela insisted they hurry to the gate as she brusquely grabbed her bag from the back seat. Once in the waiting area, Angela wouldn't sit. She paced back and forth, walking the long corridor, imploring Micki to keep her company.

When the flight was announced, Angela crossed her fingers, kissed Micki goodbye.

"When should I call you?" she asked.

"Tonight, Angela. I've got a dozen appointments today and I don't want you getting frantic if you can't reach me. How about eleven? Or later? This isn't going to be an early night for you, my love. You are going to be wined and dined New York style."

Angela squeezed Micki's arm. "You think everything's going to be all right?"

"I know it is." She brushed a wisp of curly dark hair back from Angela's forehead. "I'm very proud of you."

"That's important to me...I'll call you tonight...maybe earlier than eleven. You aren't going out, are you? You'll be home, won't you?"

"Of course."

Angela looked at the ticket as she heard the flight being announced one more time.

Micki reached out, hugged her, then quickly pushed her away. "Good luck, sweetheart."

"Love you," Angela whispered.

"Love you, too," Micki replied.

From her window seat, Angela glanced at the terminal one last time as the DC-10 began its rapid taxi down the runway. Ahead, the harbor and skyline were bathed in the brilliance of a crimson sun, banks of morning clouds were silvered by the light. She looked at her watch. Not bad; the departure delay was less than a half hour. By now, she mused, Micki would have inched her way back through the Callahan Tunnel, onto Storrow Drive, and was quite possibly already back in the apartment. Thinking of Micki made her feel confident in all that was ahead for the two of them. She felt sure that eventually she'd convince her to relocate in New York. But for the time being, they'd manage.

She recalled last night's conversation with Micki, how happy she was that Angela would know the success she'd aspired to. Soothing words comforted Angela, had allowed her to sleep through the night.

At the takeoff, the moment she perceived the beginning of the ascent, Angela gripped the arms of her seat, closed her eyes, said a silent prayer. When the plane reached its flying altitude, she looked out on the clear blue sky, smelled fresh coffee brewing, leaned back in her seat and relaxed as she looked forward to having a cup.

The pilot announced that the plane was flying over Hartford when tingling sensations began to dance lightly over Angela's hands, settling in her fingertips, prickling her skin from the inside out. Confused, pulsating, blurring images began to drum against her eyes, fears erupted out of nowhere. Micki had made it *sound* like everything would work out, but would it? What if the therapist wanted Micki to break things off? What else could they be talking about? Why *did* she spend so much time with Beverly Keating? What was behind that? Angela felt light-headed, giddy, short of breath. She wanted to drive this floating anxiety away. Reaching into her purse, she pulled out a compact, saw the capsules in the powder compartment, and selected two. Just enough to calm her, nothing more. She washed the Valium down with cold coffee, closed her eyes, and waited for the glow she knew she could count on. Soon her fears seemed no more tangible than wisps of clouds that traced the morning sky.

After they'd landed at LaGuardia, Angela was pleased to see Tom Haskell waiting for her. When he had first contacted her, she wasn't sure she needed an agent, but he'd quickly convinced her of his value when he cited a $50,000 increase he'd been able to negotiate for one of the reporters at ABC last year.

"Hardly a half hour late," he said cheerfully as he briskly stepped forward to take her bag. "We'll grab a limo and be in Manhattan by nine-thirty. You'll have time to check into your hotel, freshen up, taxi over to the network and begin what's bound to be a banner day for you."

Already, Angela was glad that he was there. A tall, lanky, red-headed man in his mid-thirties, he entertained her with a barrage of jokes and fast-paced small talk as they made their way through morning traffic into the city.

He waited with her while she checked in at the hotel, then said, "I'm going to leave you now. You'll be on your own with Donovan this morning, but I'll join the two of you for lunch. The contracts will be drawn up then, I'm sure. Any problems so far?"

"No, Tom, of course not," Angela replied in her most assured tone of voice.

"You'll do just fine and the next time I see you, we'll toast your success." In a friendly gesture, he leaned forward, kissed her on the cheek.

The hotel room was decorated in brown and sand, earth tones, accented with touches of crisp white.

"Very nice," Angela said aloud.

She decided she'd leave for the studio as soon as she unpacked. Better to be a few minutes early, she told herself. On impulse, she picked up the phone and placed a call to Hewitt's. The main number was busy, as it often was. She shrugged her shoulders, took one last look at herself in the full length mirror and dropped the room key in her purse.

Her hotel was no more than a half dozen blocks from the studio, and as Angela walked briskly down the avenue, she took in all of the excitement of the city beginning its day. She merged with the flow of foot traffic which streamed across the busy streets in obedience to the ever-changing stop lights. When she spotted the steel and glass tower of her destination, butterflies beat against her stomach. She felt a dryness in her throat. As nervous as she was, she also felt confident and sure of herself. She crossed the street, entered the building, and walked directly to the elevator.

From the moment she stepped through the large glass doors and into the studio's over-sized reception room, she was given the red carpet treatment by the network.

She was welcomed by an assistant producer and ushered into a waiting room where coffee was poured for her from a silver service. Then she was left alone for the brief time that yet remained before her interview. Eyes from five television screens stared at her from the far wall. She picked up the remote control unit, flicked from one station to another, smiled to herself. The room had been decorated in shades of ice blue and silver. A large abstract triptych dominated one of the walls, while an arrangement of smaller paintings had been hung on another. A crystal vase of fresh flowers, white gardenias and pale miniature orchids, graced a gleaming table of steel and glass.

She looked at her watch, thought about calling Micki, but decided it best to wait. Besides, she told herself, what did she have to report this early in the day?

Finally, a few minutes before eleven, Patrick Donovan's secretary paged her. She looked at her mirror, glossed her lips one last time, smoothed her hair, and stepped from the waiting room to see a giant of a man striding toward her, his hand extended to greet her.

"A pleasant flight this morning, Ms. Hall?" he asked, in a deeply resonant voice.

"Yes," she said, her voice rising with unexpected nervousness.

"What did we ever do before shuttles?"

"I don't know," she said softly, attempting to calm herself.

He smiled, held her hand in his, escorted her toward his office, gestured toward a comfortable mocha leather chair, and took a seat behind his own massive oak desk.

He leafed through papers on his desk, his manner unchanged. He crossed his arms, stared at Angela objectively at first and then quizzically, as if he were sizing her up, which he was, she realized.

He handed her a sheet of paper. "Read this for me."

She looked at the sheet and began reading copy from last night's network news broadcast.

"Not bad," he said thoughtfully, as she returned the copy.

He picked up a file folder, flipped through its pages. "You've got a good agent. Tom Haskell knows the business."

"That's what I've heard," she replied, trying to exude confidence.

He nodded, leaned forward, continued to appraise her every move.

"I like what I know about you, Angela. Boston's a hard city to work in. You've done well there, haven't you?"

"Yes," she said, hitting the right note this time.

"Any skeletons in your closet we don't know about?"

Angela smiled. "What do you mean?"

"We want our reporters coming to us clean. No scandals. No problems. Just ability and drive and a fresh shirt every night." He laughed, then his tone became serious once more, his voice hard. "Hiding anything from us?"

"No," she said indignantly, "like what?"

"Private vices. Most people have them. What are yours, Angela?"

"I don't know what you mean," she answered sharply. "I'm a reporter. A good one. What else matters?"

"I like your confidence, but I don't want any surprises once the contract's signed," he said emphatically.

"There won't be any," she assured him.

Angela found it difficult to maintain her composure in the midst of all of this, but when Donovan leaned back in his chair, propped his legs on the desk, folded his hands behind his head, she told herself that the worst of it must be over.

She was right. Donovan smiled at her broadly, then clapped his hands as if in approval.

"I like you, Hall," he said enthusiastically. "I think you're going to do a *fine* job for us. What I want us to do now is to take a look at some of your tapes. You tell me which ones you think are the best."

Donovan dimmed the lights, pressed a button on his desk and a wooden panel slid back to reveal a large screen. They spent the better part of an hour viewing Angela's broadcasts, from her first pieces for Channel 8, to her recent coverage of the protests at the nuclear power plant in Seabrook.

She explained which she thought were the most successful stories and why. It was much easier talking to Donovan in the dark, she reflected.

When they finished viewing the tapes, he said, "Haskell and I may have a few fine points to discuss, but I don't anticipate any problems with your contract." He passed the thick sheaf of typed pages across the desk to her. "Take your time looking this over, I think you'll find it's acceptable." Angela smiled confidently as she began to read the terms of the contract. Tom Haskell promised the moon, she thought exuberantly, but I never *dreamed* I'd get it.

"Presuming you'll join us on June first," Donovan said assuredly, "your salary of $300,000 will come up for review May of next year. If all goes well, it's reasonable to anticipate an increase."

"I promise you all *will* go well," Angela said happily.

She continued to read the contract, turning the pages quickly, finding it difficult to believe her good fortune. It was hard to present a calm exterior when she felt like running around the room, jumping up and down for joy, but she did her best to control herself.

"You'd sign on for nothing but a chance at the big time right now, wouldn't you?" Donovan asked. "In a while that will fade and you'll feel you're worth the small fortune we're paying you. You'll probably think you're worth even *more*," he said expansively. Then he chuckled, walked over to Angela, shook her hand.

"Welcome aboard," he said.

"Thank *you*," she replied in delight.

"And are you ready to move to New York?"

"As soon as I find an apartment," she said agreeably.

Donovan's secretary tapped on the door, ushered Tom Haskell into the office. Business was conducted quickly and with all points agreed upon, copies of the contract would be ready to sign later that afternoon. Right now, Donovan was hungry.

"Shall we escort Ms. Hall to the Four Seasons, Tom? After all," he said, "it's not every day a reporter signs a network contract."

When they entered the impressively designed restaurant, Donovan boasted, "This establishment bears the artistic stamp of two great architects, Philip Johnson and Mies van der Rohe. I dare say there's not another restaurant in the city that can make a similar claim."

They were escorted into the grand dining room and seated at a table near the pool, its clear waters shimmering in the soft light.

Almost immediately, Angela excused herself. She couldn't wait any longer, she had to tell Micki the good news. She located a telephone and using her credit card called Hewitt's. She was relieved that the line wasn't busy; the main number was ringing.

She asked the operator for Micki's extension and impatiently clicked her fingernails against the phone while she waited for an answer. Then she asked for Micki's secretary.

"Hi Meg, is Micki around?" Angela asked excitedly. "I know she said she was going to be busy today, but I thought I'd try to catch her--"

"Micki? No," Meg replied, "she didn't come in today. She called first thing this morning to say that something unexpected had come up--"

"That can't be--she said she had important meetings today."

"That's right, she did. I rescheduled them for next week. Everything all right, Angela?"

There was silence and then Angela spoke. "I'm fine," she said in a flat voice. "I'll reach her at home."

Angela made the second call, pressed the familiar numbers. She listened impatiently as the phone rang: eight, nine, ten, eleven.

She looked at her watch. It was one o'clock.

What could have come up, she asked herself.

She tried the number once more. Again, there was no answer. She jammed the plastic credit card into her jacket pocket, ducked into the Ladies room, took out her compact and impulsively tossed down the red uppers. She regretted taking so many but felt she'd need a bottle of them to bounce her up from the despair she was feeling. Her mind was clouded by the doubts she'd had earlier that morning. I was right, she thought. I was right.

For a second she wanted to enter the main lobby and leave, but she turned quickly in the direction of the dining room and walked stiffly to the table.

Patrick Donovan had ordered a bottle of wine to suit the occasion. As the waiter arrived at their table with a vintage Pouilly Fuisse, Angela excused herself again.

She leaned against the wall behind the telephone. Where could she be? What could have happened? Angela called home again. As before, there was no answer.

She phoned Hewitt's once more, asked for the advertising department.

"I'd like to speak to Beverly Keating," she said coolly.

"Bev? She's taken the day off. Anything I can help you with?"

Angela hung up the phone. She returned to the table, distracted and disbelieving of the conclusions she was quickly drawing.

"Anything wrong?" Donovan asked.

"What's happened, Angela?" Tom Haskell asked.

Angela grimaced, shook her head quickly, in anger.

"Angela," he said in a louder voice, "are you okay?"

She nodded yes.

Pat Donovan raised his glass. "To your success, Angela."

Tom raised his as well, smiled, encouraged Angela with a friendly pat on the hand to enjoy the occasion.

At that moment, however, Angela felt that she was miles away from all that was happening in this restaurant. Nevertheless, she did as she was beckoned. She raised her glass. She smiled. She drank the wine.

"If our legal department operates as it usually does," Donovan said, "those contracts won't be ready before three. You in a hurry, Tom?"

"Not at all, Pat."

"And why should you be? This represents a good day's work for us all, doesn't it? How about you, Angela? We're not holding you up, are we? I know you're having dinner with Eckhart and Morell tonight, but do you have any other engagements this afternoon?"

"No," she said, laboring to concentrate on his words.

"What's the problem, Angela? I know I was pretty rough on you today, but I had to be. I want the *best* from you; I know you can deliver."

"I just don't know *why* she's not at work," Angela continued in a high pitched voice, her words running together as her thoughts raced to conclusions she was making. "She told me she had appointments all through the morning, meetings in the afternoon--"

"Who?" Donovan asked.

Her voice like ice, she said, "My lover."

Donovan looked at Haskell, tried to digest what he was hearing.

"This is not okay," Donovan said decisively, "We can't take on this kind of...instability, Tom."

Angela reached for her glass and gulped the wine, drinking rapidly to fight back tears. Tom was talking to her. She could see the concern in his eyes, but she couldn't hear his words. She felt lost in a sea of voices.

She'd been betrayed. The faith Angela had in Micki, her trust, the *need* she had to believe in her, slipped away.

"Why is she *doing* this?" Angela asked. "Why today? I *know* they're together! She's cheating on me, she's going to leave me." Anger surfaced, control disappeared. She glared first at Tom and then at Pat Donovan. "Why?"

Haskell bent toward her, whispered sharply, "Get *hold* of yourself!"

"She thinks I don't know about it." Angela felt vindicated by the conclusions she'd drawn. She laughed cynically as she continued, "She didn't think I'd find out."

Donovan looked at Haskell, shook his head once. He had made his decision. "She's in another world, Tom. You'd better do something."

"Angela, snap out of it!" Tom shook her shoulder, but she shrugged his hand away.

"Help her out of here, Tom, *now,* before there's a scene. I'm going back to my office."

He motioned for the waiter, asked for the check, and quickly walked away.

With Donovan gone, Tom turned on Angela. "Do you *know* what you've just done? You've blown the chance a thousand reporters would have given their eye teeth for! You've ruined my credibility with Pat Donovan. He'll never want to see another client I represent! You've thrown your career away today, know that? And for what? For *who*?"

"Why would she do it?" Angela asked insistently. "Why?"

Disgusted, Tom Haskell pushed his chair back, left the table.

The waiter stepped over and spoke softly, "Is everything all right, miss?"

Angela shook her head back and forth. "No, no, no," she said dully. "Nothing's all right. Nothing."

She took a cab directly to the airport and waited in line impatiently for the first available flight, the five o'clock shuttle to Boston. She looked at her watch and saw it wasn't even three. It would be a long two-hour wait. All that she wanted was to go home. She headed for the bar, ordered a vodka on the rocks, then another.

By the time the plane landed, Angela felt in control of the situation. A few more bennies on the return flight had helped clear her confusion. As she got into the cab, she remembered she hadn't gone back to the hotel to check out.

"It doesn't matter," she said out loud.

Angela paid the cab driver, then headed toward their building. She opened the door to the lobby, reached for her key to unlock the front door. She waited patiently for the elevator, got out, and walked calmly to their door.

When she opened the door, she saw no one, though she heard voices coming from another room. Then Micki stepped from the kitchen, a bottle of wine and two glasses in her hands.

"Is that our celebration drink?" Angela asked, her voice a lament. "Guess I came back too soon." She sat down heavily on the sofa, stared across the room into nowhere.

"What are you *doing* here?" Micki asked, her expression incredulous.

"I live here," she said softly, "I live here, don't I?"

No more than seconds passed before Angela heard Micki speak again, but in that frozen shard of time, all that had happened that day went through her mind.

And then she saw Beverly Keating step from the kitchen with a plate of sandwiches.

"What happened in New York?" Micki asked, her voice a hoarse whisper. "What about the job?"

"I'm going now, Micki," Beverly said softly, "I'll call you tomorrow."

Angela looked up, sighed. "Tell her right now, Micki, that whatever's been going on between you two is finished."

"Don't be ridiculous," Micki protested, "*nothing* is going on. I felt anxious today, uneasy with you gone. I called in sick and on impulse asked Bev to keep me company for a while, until I heard from you." She looked to Beverly for confirmation, but she had already gone.

"Angela," she asked sorrowfully, "what *happened* today? What went wrong?"

"You," Angela said bluntly. "You went wrong."

Angela stood, walked to the other side of the room. She could imagine Micki watching the plane move slowly down the runway in the clear, early morning light. She could see her turn to walk back through the airport, the long corridors empty, save for vending machines and phones, endless rows of telephones. Just before passing through the last double glass door leading to the parking lot, she could see Micki pause before one last phone, could see her reach into her pocket for a handful of coins and dial Beverly's number.

"Why?" she asked.

In her mind, Angela visualized two pendulums swinging back and forth through time, not synchronized, yet keeping a crazy time with each other, nonetheless. If they collide, Angela asked, what then?

The afternoon had faded, she thought dully. The long-awaited day had finally ended. She watched distant stars appear on the horizon as a crescent moon climbed the cloudless sky. She turned to Micki, her words a chilling accusation, "You don't *know* what love is, Micki. Do you?"

"You're making too much of this," Micki pleaded.

Angela felt a wall of anger explode inside her. "Don't tell me what I'm making too much of," she screamed. "Don't tell me anything!"

Micki began to walk toward Angela, but Angela waved her back with a sweep of her arm.

"Everything went fine in New York, Micki." She seemed calm now, her tone sweet, mellow, matter of fact. "So fine that I called your office to tell you the good news. You weren't there, but you know that, of course. Then I called here. No answer. I called *her* office. She had taken the day off. I called home *again*... "The phone rang and rang and rang...couldn't you have at least answered the telephone?" she asked sadly.

"We took a walk along the river," Micki said flatly. "And you lost the job because of *that*?"

"No, I lost the job because I couldn't trust you--"

"Your career--it will take years to get to--"

Angela continued, ignoring Micki's halting words. "All my life people have left me. My mother...then my father...why should it be any different with you?"

"It will be," Micki said with conviction, "I promise."

"Yes," Angela agreed, "it will be *now*, I know."

"I'm so sorry, Angela."

Micki tried again to reach out for Angela, but Angela turned away, as if concentrating on something she saw from the window. Micki noticed nothing but the new moon, an icy sliver shining in the night sky.

Her voice soft, her tone soothing, she tried to comfort Angela. "I haven't failed you, darling, believe me. And there *will* be other chances for you. I'll make sure there will be. I'll call your agent tomorrow, smooth things over for you. It was my fault...I see that now...all my fault."

Micki sat down, a sick expression on her face, as she absorbed the impact of her own words. Why had she assumed the guilt? *Did* she believe Angela's failure had been her fault? She turned the questions over in her mind, but at this moment, there were no answers to be found. She was sure of only one thing.

"I don't want to lose you, Angela," she said passionately. "You've got to understand that."

Angela stared at Micki, her eyes cold, her lips frozen in a smile. "We'll never part, Micki. Not now. Today was just a mistake. We both made mistakes. We'll make them up to each other."

She walked to Micki, her arms open wide. As she spoke, her words ran together like syrup. "Come into the bedroom with me, hold me. I feel so safe in your arms. I'm tired now, I need to sleep. Tomorrow everything will be better for us."

"I'll make it all up to you," Micki promised, holding her close. She agreed that what they needed most was rest, that the past twelve hours would be forgotten in sleep, like a bad dream.

Angela pulled back from the embrace, "I need a shower first," she said, shaking her head groggily. "It'll help clear my mind."

In the shower, Angela watched curiously as the water streamed from the shower head, splashed on her body. She wondered why she couldn't feel it. She giggled as she rubbed soap over what she knew was her own body, though she felt absolutely nothing. It was pleasant to think of slipping over into the void, she mused, but not yet, not now.

Once out of the shower, she removed a packet taped to the bottom of her vanity drawer. She opened the small envelope, the last of her coke supply. She shook the white powder onto a mirror and smiled as she saw that she'd enough for five...maybe even six...lines.

Angela entered the room a few moments later, a large turquoise towel wrapped around her body. With her right hand, she fluffed dampness from her hair.

"Just like you said, things are going to be fine," she said liltingly, kissing Micki on the lips, bidding her to taste beads of water still on her face.

"Are you all right?" Micki asked, apprehensive that Angela had taken something, but not wanting to introduce another source of conflict.

"Of course, darling, I'm just tired...you know how that is, don't you?"

She reached for the wine, filled a glass, drank deeply.

Then she laughed as she looked at the outfit she'd worn to New York. The clothes she'd chosen so carefully were in a careless heap on the floor. She thought about picking up the suit, at least hanging the jacket over the back of a chair, arranging her skirt and blouse over that. And the shoes...they were scuffed now...she didn't like them.

As if Micki could read her mind, she began gathering Angela's clothes, but Angela had lost interest in it all, walked into the bedroom, closed the door...

Angela's suit and blouse were folded loosely over Micki's arm when she opened the bedroom door, then stepped back in shock.

"What are you doing with that gun?" she asked fearfully.

"I'll make sure you never leave me," Angela crooned, "make sure you never betray me again--"

"I never *have* betrayed you," Micki said slowly, directly, knowing she had to control the situation.

"Are you sure?" Angela asked. She held the gun loosely in her hand, smiled, then her arm dropped to her side. "I'm glad," she said peacefully. "You look beautiful to me right now, so beautiful..."

Micki reached for the gun, tried to take it, but Angela pushed her hand away, tightened her grip on the weapon.

"Angela," Micki commanded, "if you won't give the gun to me, put it back where you found it. Then come to bed. We need each other now."

Angela shook her head. "Not yet," she said quietly.

Micki reassuringly caressed Angela's shoulders, but as she reached for her hand once more, Angela moved away.

"I'm not afraid of you, Angela," she said calmly, "or of what you *think* you're going to do. I know you won't do it. We have too much to live for, the two of us. Don't throw it away because of what happened today."

Angela stepped forward, nudged the revolver against Micki's stomach. "What does that feel like, Micki?"

"Cold...lifeless...useless," she responded, grasping Angela's wrist, trying to control her own growing sense of panic.

Angela pulled away, dropped the grey, lethal weapon into the palm of her hand, looked at it one last time, and finally laid it on the

bedside table. She reached for Micki's hands; took them in her own.
"Do you want me?" she asked plaintively.

"Of course," Micki whispered.

"Forever?"

"Yes," Micki answered fervently.

"Forever," Angela repeated slowly, "I'm glad...but why am I so
tired,   Micki...I   shouldn't   be...help   me,   Micki...I'm   falling
asleep...dreaming...help me out of the dream..."

"It's   time   to   sleep,   darling...time   to   dream," Micki said
reassuringly, relieved that Angela's exhaustion had finally caught up
to her. She wasn't sure of what would come next for the two of them,
what *could* come next, but she *had* to believe that somehow they could
move forward. "Tomorrow we'll put it all back together, I promise
you..."

*****

The last week of June was a scorcher. All week long, the air
had been hot and sticky in Provincetown. Most of the time, it was
even too hot to go to the beach, unless it was to go in for frequent
swims.

Jessie and Noelle sat at the bar of the Blue Moon, idling away
the time Noelle had left before her nine o'clock show. Beverly's phone
call that afternoon had surprised them. Neither woman knew her very
well, though they'd all met on several occasions through Micki. Now
they waited for her arrival from Boston.

Jessie touched Noelle's shoulder affectionately. "Are you all
right?" she asked gently.

"I think so," Noelle answered, "a little tired, that's all."

"It's more than that," Jessie prodded.

Noelle nodded her assent and smiled. "Do you remember that
Micki herself was here last year, a little earlier in the season, perhaps,
but I know it was the month of June. That's when she first met
Angela." She paused, finding it difficult to discuss all that had

happened. "Tonight it seems that Bev is Micki's proxy...doesn't that seem eerie to you?"

"Not especially," Jessie answered, "I want to hear all that Beverly has to tell us."

"She'll arrive soon enough," Noelle answered softly.

Finally, Bev Keating entered the bar. She walked toward them slowly. After exchanging hellos, an awkward silence hung in the air, then Lana waved a friendly hello and strolled their way.

"Nice to see you back in P-town, Bev," she said warmly. "Ruth's forecast for the weekend is a ten all the way, so enjoy yourself!"

"Thanks," Bev replied, "I'm sure I will. Say Lana, any chance of a fresh cup of coffee?"

Lana glanced at the coffee maker. "So fresh it's still brewing," she beamed. "The first cup is yours. Jessie and Noelle, want a refill?"

"Sure do," Jessie answered for the two of them.

After Lana brought the coffees and moved on to other customers, Bev turned to Jessie and Noelle. There was a sad expression in her eyes.

"How's Micki doing?" Noelle inquired softly.

"Just about as you might expect," she answered thoughtfully. "Micki will come back to P-town, though I'm not sure it will be this summer. She wants to be alone right now, but when I told her I was driving down, she asked me to come to see you, to tell you what she's not able to talk about yet."

Hesitantly, Jessie spoke. "I've never been close to Micki, the way you and Noelle are, and I hardly knew Angela, but I never thought it would end the way it did. Is that naive of me to say?"

"Not really. No one could have thought of such an ending," Beverly replied.

"Lana?" Jessie responded.

"Did we ever take her seriously? And what if we had? Would it have changed anything?" Noelle asked, turning to Beverly, wanting to hear the details of the story.

"I'm glad you're here, Bev," she continued. "These past weeks, I've felt that I've had only pieces of a puzzle I couldn't complete."

"Well, I think Micki knew that and that's why she asked me to see you," Bev replied. "The day Micki saw Angela off at the airport, she crumbled. She called me, said she needed some support that day, someone to comfort her. As strange as it sounds, she couldn't get through the day without Angela...

"Of course, I went right over and listened as she spoke of her fears of losing Angela, of her inability to see a way to a future they *could* have. Micki was desperate to make it work. And it wasn't *just* the move Angela was making to New York. Micki needed to see her way, to see *their* way to a life that was less chaotic. Several times that afternoon she told me that it just *had* to work out for them in a *smoother* way...

"Micki was seeking a calm river bed. The course they'd been on had too many curves, the waters were too swift. Micki wanted to *change* that...she wanted tranquility...peace that perhaps never would have been possible with Angela. Instead they were drawn into that turbulent whirlpool...

"I was pretty sure that when Angela arrived at the apartment she had been taking *something*. I assumed that it was obvious to Micki, too, though Micki never did come to grips with Angela's use of drugs. Even Dr. Trager, the therapist Micki'd begun seeing, couldn't seem to make her deal with the seriousness of the problem. Maybe she knew and didn't want to believe. If she had, things might have been different in the morning, but who knows?

"When Micki woke up the next morning and found that Angela wasn't breathing, she called the police, then phoned me. Medics arrived at the same time I did. To get into the apartment, they had to break the door down and..."

"Please," Noelle urged, "tell us, I know how hard this must be for you."

"They found Micki in a frenzy, crying, cradling Angela in her arms." Bev shook her head in anguish and stared into the darkness of a far corner across the room. But knowing the story had to be completed, she continued. "The results of the autopsy revealed amphetamines, barbiturates, cocaine, and alcohol she'd drunk during the day. She died in her sleep, you know...peacefully...and she was where she wanted to be...in Micki's arms."

It seemed a long time before Noelle spoke. When she did her voice was choked. "Micki won't talk about it?" she asked sadly.

"She talks *around* it," Bev said quietly, "zeros in on a particular moment, then backs away from it all.

"She knows the drugs and alcohol could have had a fatal effect at any time, but she feels such guilt. Micki blames herself...feels responsible for not being more alert about what she should have known...what she says now she even suspected that night, that Angela *was* on something...and I..." Beverly's voice trailed off, her eyes filled with tears.

Noelle tried to comfort Bev, remembering how distraught she had been at the funeral last month.

"I accused myself for not staying at Micki's when Angela first returned, for not calling Micki later to see if she needed help. I still ask myself if it would have changed anything," she said angrily.

"Not too long ago, Micki talked to Tom Haskell. He was able to tell her some of what had happened that day in New York. But information doesn't necessarily provide answers," Bev reflected. "There are too many times, too many occasions when there *are* no answers, but that doesn't stop the questions from being asked...over and over again."

"Your friendship is more important to her than ever, Bev," Noelle reassured her "and Micki certainly couldn't have come as far as she has without her therapist's support. But the healing is going to take such a long time. I can't help hoping that one day soon she'll meet someone solid, someone who can take care of her."

"Someone like you," Jessie said.

"I feel very close to Micki," Beverly asserted, "and I certainly want to be there for her. Perhaps in time it will happen."

Noelle thought about all that Beverly had said, told herself that she wanted to see Micki soon, wanted to see if she and Jessie could help her through the endless process of grief and mourning. At the very least, it would give Micki a chance to talk once more about Angela... Noelle knew that for now, at least, the story had ended.

As sad as she felt for Micki, she also felt strangely haunted by Angela.

She'd been judged harshly by many, Noelle thought...and loved by only one.

For all of her problems, her insecurities, the complications of her life, Noelle knew that none of them would ever forget her.

She reached out for Beverly's hand, for Jessie's as well. "I want to call Micki tomorrow," she said. "Bev, will you come by, help me find the words...it's still so hard to know what to say."

Beverly returned her affectionate clasp, "Yes," she said. "We'll do it together."

Biographical Sketch of Authors

Shelley Smith is the pseudonym of two writers who live outside of Boston. They feel that *Edge of Passion*, their third collaborative work, explores more serious themes than previous novels, *Horizon of the Heart* and *The Pearls*.

The authors' backgrounds and interests are diverse. Work experience includes editing, advertising copywriting, free-lance writing and teaching, for one of the partners. The other has had a career in interior design and various phases of real estate management. They are enthusiastic travelers, sailors and gardeners, and have raised children, as well as numerous cats and dogs. At present, they are working on their fourth novel.

ROMANCING THE DREAM

H.H. Johanna

Author and journalist, H.H. Johanna, makes her debut as a novelist with **Romancing the Dream**--a captivating and erotic love story--with an unusual twist.

This imaginative tale begins when Jacqui St. John leaves northern California looking for a new home, and cruises into the seemingly ordinary town of Kulshan. Seeing the lilac bushes blooming along the roadside, she suddenly remembers the recurring dream that has been tantalizing her for months--a dream of a house full of women, radiating warmth and welcome, and of one special woman dressed in silk and leather.

But why has Jacqui, like so many other women, been drawn to this town? And what is the secret of the women of Kulshan?

Romancing the Dream (176 pages; $8.95) is another novel from **Rising Tide Press**, and is available at your local women's bookstore or directly from the publisher. Send your order to **Rising Tide Press**, 5 Kivy Street, Huntington Station, NY 11746. Please be sure to enclose $8.95 plus $3.50 for shipping and handling.

FREE
LESBIAN MAIL ORDER
BOOK CATALOG

We Offer:

- Over 1000 books, videos, records
- Toll-free ordering
- Fast, personal service
- Discreet mailing
- Phone orders welcome! Charge it on Mastercard or Visa.

Send for your FREE CATALOG today.

Womankind Books
5 Kivy Street · Dept RTP
Huntington Station, NY 11746
1-800-648-5333

Please send 2 stamps with request for catalog.

RISING TIDE PRESS

OUR PUBLISHING PHILOSOPHY

Rising Tide Press is a Lesbian-owned and operated publishing company committed to publishing books for, by and about Lesbians, and their lives. We are not only committed to readers, but also to Lesbian writers who need nurturing and support, whether or not their manuscripts are accepted for publication. Through quality writing, the press aims to entertain, educate, and empower readers, whether they are women-loving-women or heterosexual. It is our intention to promote Lesbian culture, community, and civil rights, nationwide, through the printed word.

In addition, RTP will seek to provide readers with images of Lesbians aspiring to be more than their prescribed roles dictate. The novels selected for publication will aim to portray women from all walks of life, (regardless of class, ethnicity, religion or race), women who are strong, not just victims, women who can and do aspire to become more, and not just settle, women who will fight injustice with courage. Hopefully, our novels will provide new ideas for creating change, in a heterosexist and homophobic society. Finally, we hope our books will encourage Lesbians to respect and love themselves more, and at the same time, convey this love and respect of self to the society at large. It is our belief that this philosophy can best be actualized through fine writing that entertains, as well as educates the reader. Books, even Lesbian books, can be fun, as well as liberating.

If you share our vision of a better Lesbian future, and would like to become a part of a network helping to promote these publishing goals, please consider making a contribution, any amount appreciated, to Rising Tide Press, so that we may continue this important work into the future.

RISING TIDE PRESS

Writers Wanted!!!

Rising Tide Press, Publisher of Lesbian Novels is Soliciting Quality Fiction Manuscripts

Rising Tide Press is interested in publishing quality Lesbian fiction: romance; mystery; and science fiction. Non-fiction is also welcome, but please, no poetry or short stories. Send us the following:

1. One page synopsis of plot.
2. The manuscript.
3. Large brown envelope with return postage.
4. A brief autobiographical sketch.

5 KIVY ST., HUNTINGTON STA., NY 11746 (516) 427-1289